A WAYFARING STRANGER

Tormented by visions, middle of a barren a yellow-toothed g this country's high believes will lead he

...ring
...ong that she
...er other self.

A CHURCH IN THE
MIDDLE OF NOWHERE

Held captive in a desecrated shrine, Celia would have given up long ago if not for a song that keeps her hope burning. Someday she will escape from the shadowy creatures that claw at the windows of the church, the monstrous dog with a taste for human flesh, and the old preacher with inhuman powers.

A BOND THAT
CROSSES WORLDS

Two women divided by fate but connected by blood. Will the song help them lead the way to each other and defeat the forces aligned against them? Or will they suffer the dreadful fate of...

THOSE WHO FOLLOW

PRAISE FOR THE SISTERS OF SLAUGHTER

Mayan Blue
2016 Nominee - Bram Stoker Award for Superior Achievement in a First Novel.

"A brilliantly imagined, comprehensively researched vision of hell done up the Mayan way, replete with owl-headed gods, shapeshifting demons, and a whole host of other creatures both terrible and wonderful." – *This is Horror*

"I was expecting something dripping with gore and I wasn't disappointed." – *Grim Reader Reviews*

"The Sisters of Slaughter live up to their moniker with blood-soaked scenes of brutality and some pretty nightmarish creatures. Seriously, this novel is loaded with so many terrifying creatures, it is a horror fan's dream!" – *The Horror Bookshelf*

"These two show no quarter dragging the characters– and by extension, the reader–into the depths of the Mayan version of Hell. There's vividness to the scenes they craft that made me want to make sure I was reading in full daylight, or at least with most of the lights on." –*John Quick, Author of Consequences*

"Stephen King, R.L. Stine, watch out! Michelle Garza & Melissa Lason are a horrific match, a deadly duo!" – *iHorror.com*

<u>Also from Michelle Garza and Melissa Lason</u>

<u>Novels</u>

Mayan Blue (from Sinister Grin Press)

Short Stories

Double Barrel Horror: Just a Few/Tenant's Rights

THOSE WHO FOLLOW

by Michelle Garza
& Melissa Lason

READ UNTIL YOU BLEED!

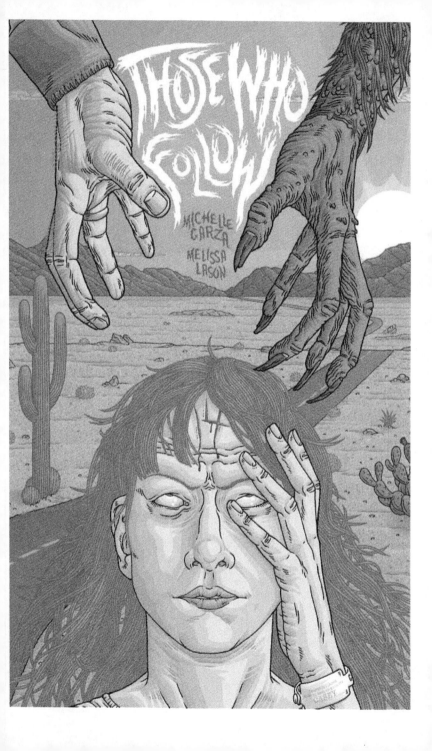

PROLOGUE

A CHURCH IN THE MIDDLE OF NOWHERE

The sun seemed unusually bright above her, even for Arizona. Luckily for her, it was only mid-April and the summer heat had yet to take hold in the desert. The highway looked like a black river of dried asphalt with the customary adornment of broken yellow lines—a highway like any other she had seen and yet it felt foreign to her all the same. She guessed that she had fallen asleep in that old man's front seat and must've worn out her welcome because the last thing she could recall was watching the moon through the windshield of that old car; it was riding high in a clear desert sky with its light falling softly on the miles of barren land below. She was now walking along the roadside in broad daylight wondering where she was. She felt her pockets for fear that she had been rolled but found all her belongings in place. She swung the lightweight pack from her shoulder and inspected its contents to find everything still there.

"Must've blacked out again." Celia spoke her thoughts out loud.

She had a habit of doing that, imbibing a little too much of the flask in her bag or swallowing a few too many of the assortment of pills that had become her only companions on the road and losing a few hours, a few days.

There wasn't a sign of life around and so she continued on her present course in hopes of spotting an oncoming vehicle that she could thumb down. Maybe catch a ride up north and spend the summer there amongst the ponderosa pine trees. Her mother had often complained about her nomadic lifestyle but to Celia it was the ultimate freedom, living off the grid, drifting around like a feather on the breeze. She was lost in an imaginary argument with the old woman whose repetitive criticism about hiking around in the middle of nowhere and accepting rides from strangers was met with Celia's repetitive answer, the same she had flung at her mother since she was seventeen and started her roaming.

"You have never lived, only existed. You don't know what it is to experience anything because you hide in your house afraid of everything. That's not for me!"

The old woman couldn't answer her now or ever again seeing how she had been dead for three years, but, in Celia's moments of self-doubt, she chose to lash out at the memory of her mother instead of herself. She would always squeeze the side pocket of her back pack to locate the tiny jewelry box that her mother had given her as a gift and let the old woman have it.

She stood for a moment and looked about. The deserts on the roadsides were akin to those of higher elevations and she wondered how far the old man had taken her before deciding to ditch her unconscious on the roadside. She was irritated yet relieved that she hadn't woken up to find him groping her. Her concentration was broken by a rumbling in the distance and thought a thunderhead may be building up, so she continued her wandering. She could see a thicket of mesquite trees up the road and thought she might rest there. It would be the only reprieve from the rain, if it came.

Celia made it to her only oasis as the scent of rain filled her nose, carrying with it the smell of wet creosote bushes and she knew the storm would be on her soon. She leaned her back against the rough bark of a mesquite tree and instantly shot from her seat. She swatted at her back that was now burning and irritated, her panic growing until she was certain that no scorpions had crawled down her shirt. She contorted her head as far as it would turn on her neck and inspected what appeared to be a crescent shaped cut. The humidity was building with the approaching storm and her sweat had gotten into the wound. She sighed heavily, relieved that she wouldn't need to worry about seeking medical attention on top of her present set of needs, that consisted of finding another soul that could either offer her shelter for the night or a ride to a place that could provide it. Her thoughts were broken by the sound of music in the distance and she grinned, hoping her troubles had all been resolved.

Beyond the thicket of mesquite trees there was a dirt road that bisected the main highway and she followed it in hopes of finding some folks. On down the road, she could see a wooden building and she quickened her pace as a light spattering of rain fell down to speckle the dirt road and the lonely girl that walked it.

As she drew near, she realized that the building was a dilapidated church and she paused, looking down at her cut-off jean shorts, tank top and combat boots, worried that the church going types may not receive her well, but she pushed that concern aside.

The shape of the building, with its steeple leaning unsteadily, and dust-covered windows would have caused her to believe it was abandoned if it weren't for the music.

Another thought blossomed in her mind. Perhaps it was a flop house for other drifters. The prospects of possibly finding some other free spirits sent her quickly forward, hoping they were in a sharing mood and that she could replenish her stock of booze and pills. Her confusion and rising apprehension over feeling lost for the first time in years was cast aside and she grinned as she stepped foot on the first rickety step that led up to the church door.

The music was that of a church organ, yet instead of inspiring the Holy Spirit within her, it made her think of those bands from the sixties and seventies and made her hope the inhabitants of the church also doled out hallucinogens. Her heavy boots bowed the wooden steps as she ascended them slowly and, as she reached the door, the music died so suddenly she flinched at the still silence that engulfed her. There wasn't a bird in the sky. Not an insect came to inspect the perspiration that was now gathering in her underarms. The measly storm had petered out and left only its humidity as a reminder that it had rolled through at all. A second steady rumble behind her caused her to pause, for it wasn't the sound of any storm but that of an engine and it roused such a sense of déjà vu that her body reacted before her brain could make sense of sudden terror that sent her sprinting around the side of the church in the middle of nowhere.

She watched from her hiding spot as the shining front end of a black car came into view and her vision blurred. A swooning feeling came over her and the threads of a nightmare began weaving together in her mind. Her stomach knotted as if she had downed a bottle of rot-gut whiskey. Her memory was restored and she now recalled most of the happenings of the night before.

A black highway, a black car stopping beside her as she swallowed a handful of downers. The old man with a yellow toothed grin, that old cars engine roaring as if it had been completely bored out. Her apprehension steadily growing as he pressed the pedal to the floor and the effect of her narcotic dinner taking hold of her.

She could see the moon through the windshield and felt for the door handle. Celia asked kindly if she could be let out and when he turned, his eyes met hers and her stomach seized for all he did was smile and continue to push that old car to its limits. There was something not right in his eyes. They were devoid of humanity and she knew he wasn't as harmless as his age let on. He laughed and she knew that he was aware of the effect he had on her. There was a rancid panting on the back of her neck, but she dared not turn around. She pushed at the door and felt the warm desert wind on her face and a sharp pain in her back.

Celia could recall no more, but she knew that this man was someone to be feared and avoided at all costs. She crouched lower and continued to watch his approach. The car came to a stop and the driver's side door was flung open and he stepped into the sunlight. Celia could see him better now—he had white hair, tanned skin, and a sweat-stained button-down white shirt. He busied himself with opening the trunk of his car and she looked about frantically for a better place to hide, but all that stretched out for miles was lonesome desert.

She wished that she hadn't left the thicket of mesquite but she would never make it back there now. He and that black car stood between her and the withering branches of those trees. She didn't want to find herself lost in the expanses of the desert behind her. She had always considered herself streetwise, yet she was clueless as to the ways of wilderness survival and, calculating her chances of making it out of those barren lands, she knew they were extremely nil.

She looked back to see him unloading a heavy tool box and hauling it up to the steps before the church but she lost sight of him. Behind him, from the back seat of the car, came bounding a hound the likes of which she'd never seen and, as it raised its massive snout to sniff the air, her stomach knotted. The beast was the size of grown man, with a hide that was black as pitch and steady streams of thick slobber dripping from its dangling lips. A low growl started in its belly and sprung forth in a drawn-out baying as it tilted its head back and leapt forward.

Scrambling from her hiding spot, she fled, cursing her limbs that seemed atrophied with fear. A waking nightmare came bearing down on her with ungodly speed. The sound of the massive hound's paws tearing the dusty earth beneath it was second only to the thunderous pounding of her pulse in her ears. The distance between them was closed in a matter of seconds and, as it leapt, she was flooded with defeat.

She went down under its weight, the breath knocked from her instantly, and the sensation of its jaws snapping at her flesh elicited cries from her dusty throat that she knew would fall on deaf ears. Celia attempted to cover the back of her neck with her hands only to provoke the monstrous hound who reacted by latching onto her wrist and shaking her madly. She felt her petite body being tossed about without the slightest of exertion. She could hear the snapping of bones and, as her adrenaline waned, the agony of her injuries sank in.

A short whistle halted the loyal dog and it released her there in the dirt. The sun above her was blotted out by his silhouette and before she lost consciousness she looked up to see him grinning down at her with his mouth of decaying teeth.

$$\star\ \star\ \star\ \star$$

Celia could taste blood and dirt on her tongue and she opened her eyes. She felt drowsy and disoriented. Her heartbeat was slow and heavy and her mind fixated on it, for a moment worried it would stop completely. The hot panting of the hound was at her cheek, yet she didn't dare make eye contact with it. Mixed with its rancid exhalation was a smell of rot. As her mind fought to grasp the situation, her eyes began to focus and she could see the old man standing over her. Her gaze went beyond his grinning face to the dilapidated ceiling of the broken-down church. The beams were dry-rotted and splitting. Nailed to those beams were countless driver's licenses, military I.D. cards and photographs that were yellowed with time and covered in dust.

"Sixty-eight, why don't you play us a tune to mark this special occasion?" he spoke.

The church organ began to blare, startling her back to full consciousness. She was lying upon a splintering wooden altar table and out amongst the pews were two other women and one more behind the organ. The three of them wore heavy shackles and chains about their ankles. They were filthy and haggard and their eyes held a feral glare. One of them stood and lumbered past where she lay, hobbling as she dragged her chain behind her. The other woman's gnarled hands moved over the organ and an off-key rendition of the wedding march played.

Celia writhed feebly but found that her battered body had been tied down to the altar table. The music wore on until it clumsily came to its climax and he stood over her, his hands high above his head. The church walls shook with the reverberating organ music and dust motes danced in her vision.

As all fell silent he took up a knife. He kissed the blade reverently as if in some kind of blessing. He lowered it until it paused just above her forehead and he addressed the women in the pews.

"We are gathered here today to welcome number fourteen to the fold."

He brought the tip of the blade down into her flesh, scoring her forehead. Searing pain brought tears to her eyes and when her blood came fast and hot, it ran into them.

"We shall also mourn the passing of Seventy-one."

She could hear a violence in his voice as he stepped aside. Behind him was an inverted cross with the corpse of a naked women nailed to it, the number Seventy-one carved into her forehead. Celia was grateful now that her years of cocaine abuse had nearly abolished her sense of smell, yet what did seep in caused her to vomit uncontrollably.

"I don't allow such nonsense in here!"

He brought his fist down, crushing the bridge of her nose. His outburst sent the other three women cowering in the pews.

Celia swallowed her tears and wept, "OH GOD, PLEASE, JUST LET ME GO!"

"God can't hear you here. He has no power here. Ask them." He nodded to the three terrified women that huddled together. "I AM GOD. I AM THE DEVIL. THIS WORLD BELONGS TO ME AND NOW YOU DO TOO!"

Spittle hung on his lips and the blood rushed to his cheeks. His hound growled, pacing the floor, and she knew with just a whistle from its master, it would eat her alive. With a slice of his knife, he tore free a decaying slab of meat from Seventy-one's thigh and tossed it to the beast.

"Teach her the rules." He commanded the trio of mangled women whom he called his wives.

He cut Celia's bindings with his gory blade and slapped a heavy shackle around her ankle. He mopped his face with the back of his sleeve and left her there. She rolled from the altar to the splintering wooden floor. Her boots had been cut off and her pack was gone. He made his way to a coat rack beside the door and busied himself putting on a clean shirt. "Be a good dog." He smiled down affectionately at the beast as it hungrily lapped up the remainder of its putrid dinner.

The car roared to life and, through the dusty window, she watched him prepare to depart.

"Don't cry too much," said Sixty-eight. "At least he spared you, if it weren't for Seventy-one going he would have marked you as a sow."

"What does that mean?" Celia questioned.

"What do you think it means?" the monstrous woman asked. "You really can't be that dense?"

She dragged her chain along beside her and sat beside Celia who cradled her broken arm. "You would've been cut up like the others," she pointed to the ceiling and the many photos. "Fed to the dog... fed to us."

Celia looked up to the adornment of what was left of his victims.

"We can get out of here... call the police." She desperately offered.

"There is no getting out," a second wife added, rubbing the number on her forehead, eighty-two.

"There are no police. Only him. Just be thankful he is too old to consummate your marriage."

The third and last wife—ninety-seven—nodded but spoke not a word. Celia looked back to the window as the engine of that old car revved with such ferocity she thought the motor might combust. He threw it in gear and whipped the car around, kicking up rooster tails of powdery dust.

A peculiar orb of light materialized before him. It looked like ball lightening that danced with electricity and pulsed a light blue hue. It began to expand, pulling itself wider and wider until it was large enough to accommodate the old black car. In astonishment and sickening hopelessness, she watched it open. On the other side, there was a starry night sky and a stretch of highway. He flipped on his headlights and she recognized a crooked saguaro, the same cactus she had stopped beside the night she took a ride from the old man. He punched the pedal and the car was obscured in a combination of dust and white electricity that pulsed through the arid environment until it was at last swallowed up. The passageway closed in the blink of an eye, fading to nothing but a pin prick of light and then it was gone... he was gone. She was left there with the three women, those that had lost any semblance of humanity at his hands and a dog that was raised to eat human flesh.

"There isn't any way out." The old woman pointed to her forehead.

"I have been here since nineteen sixty-eight, from your marking, I take it that the year is now twenty fourteen."

Celia nodded and began shaking, weeping pitiful sobs until she hacked and gagged.

"Imagine if a gift like that had been bestowed upon a man with a kindly soul, one that could have used it in some way for the good of people, but instead it was given to such a vicious man," Sixty-eight sighed heavily.

"He could have changed the world but instead he created his own here, a place to carry out fantasies that couldn't be concealed on the other side, a place where

God and the Devil are one and the same. They are both him."

Eighty-two looked to the corpse of Seventy-one and added. "No one makes it out of here alive. She tried, but as the days go by, I wonder if a fate like hers would be so bad?"

She turned and looked to the window and spoke the very question that was passing through Celia's confused mind. "I often wonder who he is on the other side."

★ ★ ★ ★

The meatloaf was nearly finished. the mashed potatoes and green beans were warming on the stove top. She had set the table just how he liked it and smoothed her hair. She reapplied her lipstick and waited for him on the sofa. It wasn't long before she heard the rumbling of his car's engine. She grinned. It was his pride and joy. He'd had that old car since before they were married and refused to give it up, just as he refused to give up his job as a traveling antique salesman. He spent a lot of time on the road but he always provided really well for them so she never complained. She heard the jingling of his keys in the door and she stood to check her makeup once more in the mirror above the fireplace. She wasn't as attractive as she used to be but she knew that neither was he. She loved him even as his hair faded white and his teeth grew yellow, he was the gentlest man she had ever known, not a mean streak in him to be seen in all thirty-eight years of marriage. He came through the door and affectionately swept her up in his arms.

"My old Seventy-six!" he teased and held out a small jewelry box before her eyes.

"It's beautiful," she kissed his cheek and smirked. "I thought you had ran out on me with a younger woman!" she winked and marveled at the anniversary gift her loving husband had brought.

"Not in this life, darling!" he answered with a yellow-toothed grin.

CHAPTER ONE
OCTOBER, 1983

Annemarie stood with her palm against the windowpane to feel the cold transferring through it from the rain pelting the other side. It kept her mind from the searing pain building in her lower back. Her stomach tightened until it felt as if she bore a forty-pound stone beneath her skin. Her abdomen distended and rolled. She let her hand fall to feel the writhing children in her womb—*his children.*

A hand gripped her shoulder. "Let's walk for a while. It will help you to progress faster," Nurse Johnson spoke.

The tone of her voice was usually flat and emotionless when dealing with the young woman, but tonight a warmth crept into it, though it didn't quite sound completely genuine, like the voice of someone attempting to manipulate an unruly child.

A boom of thunder sent the patient fumbling in confusion as if she was waiting for something, her eyes searching the corners of the half-lit room that were obscured by darkness. Nurse Johnson figured that she must have been terrified to know that she would soon be giving birth to twins. It made the old woman cringe.

She had witnessed quite a few pregnancies, but Annemarie's had been arduous. She knew its end would undoubtedly be agony.

Annemarie shifted away from Nurse Johnson's grasp and brought her only hand up to touch her forehead, "Did you make it safe?"

"Of course, come along now."

Annemarie looked down at her left wrist. The faint feeling of a ghost limb longed to reach over and rub the bruises away from being restrained, yet her right arm had been taken nine months earlier. The storm outside rattled the walls and brought with it thoughts of the stranger and the place he had taken her—that church in the middle of nowhere.

The cold concrete beneath the soles of her bare feet agitated the cramps that had begun to tighten in her calf muscles, turning her toes up painfully. The contractions were steadily growing in ferocity and getting closer together. They exited the sitting area and turned up the long hallway leading to her room. The tile was yellowed under the hanging bulbs illuminating her path to what she knew would be her deathbed. Annemarie felt more like a death row inmate walking that last stretch before getting strapped in to ride the lightning and, strangely, she welcomed it.

She ran her hand through the hair at the side of her head. It had been shorn close to her scalp after she entered Stillwater, but now it was long enough to grip a handful of it. Her stomach hardened once more and the sting of her auburn hair coming free in her palm didn't take an ounce of the pain away. She trembled violently and cried out, wondering if her gut would just burst open, spilling the unnatural children of the stranger out on that piss-colored flooring.

Nurse Johnson walked a few steps ahead of Annemarie and when the young woman stopped, her face white and teeth clenched, her only hand tearing free hair from the abused scalp beneath, the Nurse quickly made her way to her station just a few yards away to call for Dr. Laurence. She spoke in a hushed voice, watching as her patient's nightgown became wet with blood and broken water.

"It's time. Annemarie is ready."

★ ★ ★ ★

"How did she manage to get out?" Dr. Laurence asked as he hurried up the hall, rolling his sleeves up.

"It was time, she needed to walk. I took her for a few passes around the ward." Nurse Johnson answered, her voice once more flat and monotone. "You're lucky she carried them to term."

The old battle axe had already prepared herself for what had to be done, it wasn't the first time she had taken part in such a thing, yet she knew that when she was well into the autumn years of her life, all the ghosts of these moments would be the only visitors to come to her bedside to make her recount the mistakes she had made willingly.

Anne was laid on her bed, the mattress thin and unforgiving to her aching back. They feared that tying her down to the bed would only hinder the birthing process, so they left the young woman unrestrained.

Dr. Laurence looked to his nurse, her face now filled with anxiety, something he wasn't accustomed to seeing. They just wanted it all done and behind them, to be rid of the peculiar woman and the children in her growing belly. Nurse Johnson had purposefully only alerted Dr. Laurence, leaving their colleagues to man the other floors so that he had no one there to question his decisions, no one there to show mercy to the girl that had been nothing but heartache since she had been placed in their care.

* * * *

Sweat beaded at the scar tissue on Annemarie's forehead, the number eighty-two visible in the sterile white light above them. She cried out as Nurse Johnson pulled her upper body forward to cram pillows behind her back.

"Hush," She scolded the tormented young woman.

Annemarie wanted to claw the old woman's face off when she snapped at her, as if giving birth to two demon children was no big deal. That's all they could be, just like the monster who had put them in her. She knew in her heart she should have killed them sooner, but the doctor had kept her restrained so she couldn't hurt herself or them. Anne had tried a few times, by punching herself in the stomach, swallowing pieces of broken drywall from her window sill. She had even tried throwing herself down the stairwell, but the old woman had caught her and dragged her back by the hair of her head.

Anne had been forced to watch herself change, watch them grow inside of her, beneath her skin like an infestation of some horrendous parasite. She was relieved when the doctor told her the children would go directly into the adoption program, yet she wondered if God would be angry with her for unleashing such vermin into the world—the spawn of the wanderer who drove the black car.

Dr. Laurence wheeled in a cart laden with the necessities of delivering the children. Atop it sat two cardboard boxes lined with towels. He ran his hand up between Anne's legs and nodded.

"She's almost there."

Annemarie gasped with each contraction, holding her breath against the terrible pain that tore through her insides. *They're trying to kill me... like he tried.*

An ammonia smell assaulted her nostrils, bringing bile up the back of her throat. Nurse Johnson gripped Anne's hand in her calloused palm, coaching her to push the young ones free of the birth canal. Anne felt a tearing. Hot agony erupted between her legs.

"It's not safe here! He's going to find me!" Annemarie screamed. "I can feel his eyes on me!"

"THERE ISN'T ANYONE HERE, ANNEMARIE!" Nurse Johnson said. "PUSH! GET IT DONE!"

Annemarie tried to buck and kick, yet her body would not heed her outburst.

"I can see a head. PUSH!" Dr. Laurence said.

She did as she was told. Her body was no longer her own. It hadn't been for nine months. All Annemarie wanted was to free herself of the scourge that was now fighting to break free, hoping the feeling of the stranger's hands on her would leave with his cursed seed. She pushed again, feeling something sliding out of her torn body.

Doctor Laurence lifted the child, coated in blood and white mucous, it appeared foreign though its slick hair was the same color as her own. The doctor cleared its throat and it screamed... it deafened Anne, pierced her skull between her eyes like a quick stab of an ice pick. He placed the baby in one of the boxes and returned to tend to Anne as she struggled to recover from hearing the young one's voice. It invaded her mind and left her feeling like her head would surely split in two.

The second child came after only minutes of reprieve, exhausting her to the point of losing consciousness. Its cries felt like a hammer battering against her brain.

Annemarie prayed that death would claim her then, and it didn't take long to oblige her. Nurse Johnson wheeled the crying babies from the room as Dr. Laurence stepped away, leaving Annemarie to bleed out in her bed.

CHAPTER TWO

MAY 2014

"I am a poor, wayfaring stranger,
traveling through this world alone..."

"You refuse to bathe?" he asked, looking down at the notepad in his lap. "Why?"

"We've gone over this before. I can feel someone touching me," Casey answered.

"Touching you?"

"Not sexually, if that's what you're askin'," she said. "It's like someone puttin' their arms around me."

Dr. Greenburg halted her there to jot down her response before continuing.

"You've told administration you hear voices. Do you still hear them after three weeks of being here?"

"It's not voices, it's a single voice. And yes, I do."

"And what does it say, does it tell you to do things? Did it tell you to harm your brother?"

"He's not my blood brother, he reminds me of that all the time. She sings, sometimes she talks but it's all garbled, I can't understand it."

"What does she sing?" Dr. Greenburg asked.

"Wayfaring Stranger." Casey answered.

"Does the voice ever tell you to hurt yourself?" He asked, his eyes falling on the scars on her wrists.

"No, I've only started hearing it recently, I just told you I can't understand what it's sayin'. These were from a long time ago, when I was a teenager." She pulled the sleeves of her shirt down to avert his gaze.

"How do you know it's a female voice if it's indecipherable?" He asked, already knowing her response.

"Because," She paused, feeling the dread of being labeled insane swelling up in her stomach, "I see her sometimes too."

His pen went to work, feverishly dictating her answer.

"In the mirror, she stands right behind me."

"Can she see you?" he asked.

"I don't believe so."

"She just stands behind you"

Casey nodded. "And behind her is no longer my room."

"What do you see behind her?"

"There's an old church."

"What does she look like?"

That question—she had been waiting for it.

"She looks just like me, but she's got a bleeding cut on her forehead."

"Could it be that it's a past memory?" Dr. Greenburg asked. "Something you've repressed?"

"I've never left Colorado, and she is standing in front of a church, in a desert. No, it's not me, or anything from my life."

"So these visions of another woman—"

"Another me..."

"Another you?"

"Yes." Casey said.

"What do you think is trying to be communicated to you through this other you?" He asked.

"I have no idea. Sometimes I wish she would leave me alone, but I think she's been here my whole life. Her eyes are filled with hurt and hopelessness... and I feel like... I don't know..."

"Like what?"

"So hopeless too." She answered honestly.

"Well, we are here to help you with that." He grinned.

Something in her gut told her there was nothing he could do for her at all, but she nodded and returned his smile half-heartedly.

****

John had told her she was crazy, that his mother had picked her up like a stray puppy from the adoption agency. Catherine had confirmed it on her death bed. Her whole life Casey had never felt connected to any of them... that she had never known herself at all. John hadn't provoked her just to get her sent away. It was to keep her from his mother's will. Casey sighed, if she had just stayed away from the funeral she wouldn't have found herself in a mental institution. She only went to bid Catherine farewell, the old woman deserved it after raising Casey, but John's mouth needed a good slap to silence his self-righteous ranting. All Casey could think was how she could be home, in her apartment alone... listening to her other-self sing.

The burden of knowing that her blood mother had died in an institution was something that had gnawed at her daily. Paranoia had taken root in her, causing her the terrible anxiety of wondering if she was losing her mind. She had been checked into Whispering Creek Mental Health Facility after the police heard her begging her other-self to be quiet when they came to question her about "assaulting" her brother.

Casey had admitted to seeing the woman in the mirror to another psychologist, but she had been passed on to Dr. Greenburg for more in-depth care. It was only her second session with him and already she didn't like him. He seemed like a liar like all the rest, only looking to force handfuls of pills down her throat to keep her a functioning member of society, something she honestly never wanted to be.

****

"I don't want to be a medicated zombie," she spoke.

"Don't look at it that way," Javier said as he changed the lightbulb above her bed.

"How should I look at it?" Casey asked.

"Look at it like you're on a journey and the reward is finding yourself and the happiness within," he answered.

"You don't talk like the rest of these people," Casey said.

"I don't think the same way as most of them either," he answered.

He descended his ladder and pushed the bed back into place. She sat watching him. He could see how exhausted she was.

"You're going to feel whole again," he said.

Casey smiled. Her eyes watered. "Thank you."

Javier left her there to finish his work, hoping his words were the truth.

★ ★ ★ ★

Night crawled down the walls of Whispering Creek, dragging storm clouds along with it. Lightning intermittently lit the thick windows, casting shadow puppets of the world beyond across the walls, the leafy hands of the trees taunting those who weren't free enough to sway in the storm with them but instead were locked away within those claustrophobic brick walls.

Casey waited, knowing the screams would rage through the night as the storm passed over. The other patients—those fighting their own imaginary demons—always flung themselves against their room doors during bad weather. No one dared to call them cells, not in front of the patients, though Casey knew that's exactly what they were.

Some of the patients were restrained with thick straps attached to their bedsides when they acted out. Casey tried to keep quiet, she didn't want to be tied down again, but with each flash beyond her window a slow song began to form in her mind.

★ ★ ★ ★

"Storms and full moons always make them go crazy," Alicia said.

"Crazier," Cameron corrected her, then snickered.

"Smoke break's nearly over. Are you ready to go back in?" she asked.

"I guess. I'm never ready to go in but it pays the bills," he answered in his mischievous way.

"Only seven more hours," she sighed, then flicked her cigarette out into the rain beyond the overhang.

They passed through the exit door. He kicked the heavy wooden doorstop back out onto the sidewalk and pulled it closed. Cameron pushed his hand against the door to be sure it was secured. then turned back to Alicia. "Are you ready to rumble?"

She rolled her eyes and left him staring after her. She made sure to walk with that certain strut she knew he liked to watch.

"Let me know if you need a lift home!" he called after her.

Alicia made her way to the top floor, hoping the ward nurse wouldn't complain that she smelled like cigarettes again. The screams seemed to blend in now. They used to startle her, but after two years of working there, she had become accustomed to them. Often, when she was alone, the silence of her house was nearly too quiet, causing her ears to strain for the slightest little sounds.

"Benchman is really going at it tonight," the ward nurse, Jackie, said. "He just won't stop... think it's time for Cameron to come strap him in."

Alicia felt her gut knot. Martin Benchman was by far their most violent patient. She always felt nervous when her boyfriend was called up to restrain him.

"Call for Javier too, just in case we need some extra muscle," Jackie told Alicia who lifted a walkie-talkie to her mouth.

****

Martin was in rare form, pacing his room, flipping the bed on its side with no signs of exerting himself. He wasn't a large man—his form was the opposite in fact—but his strength was nearly insurmountable when in the midst of a delusional episode. He was also legally blind so it made their approach a little easier.

Cameron unlocked the door and stepped in softly, trying not to appear like a threatening blob in Martin's hazy vision. Javier followed behind him, readying himself for one of Martin's attacks. Jackie waited, a syringe of sedative filled and ready.

"Mr. Benchman, everything is alright," Cameron spoke. "It's me, Cameron, and Javier is with me."

"NO!" Martin screamed. "LEAVE ME BE!"

"What's troubling you, my friend?" Javier asked.

They held their position as the patient kicked at his bed and punched wildly at the wall.

"Don't you hear her?" he asked.

"Hear what, Martin?" Jackie asked from her safe place behind Cameron and Javier.

"That fuckin' singing!" Martin leaned his back against the wall and slid down it to sit on the floor. "She's going to call down the apocalypse. You know that!"

He slammed the back of his head against the wall. "WE'RE ALL GOING TO DIE!"

Cameron and Javier stepped forward as Martin continued pounding his head into the bricks. In sick, muted thuds, his flesh split open, a crimson circle of blood and scalp left sticking to the cream-colored paint from his abuse.

"Stop him, Cameron!' Jackie ordered.

The orderlies handled Martin firmly yet with care. Both Javier and Cameron didn't want to intentionally harm Martin in their pursuit of stopping him from bashing his own brains out. Jackie and Alicia righted the thin patient bed and prepared to help restrain him as Cameron and Javier forced him down on top of it. Nurse Jackie administered the sedative after Mr. Benchman's wrists and ankles were restrained. He fought and bucked against the straps, spit up at Jackie and called her every filthy name in the book before the meds took hold of him.

He whimpered, a tear slid from the corner of his eye. "We're all gonna die."

"You have to relax, Martin. Nothing will happen to you or any of us. We've got Cameron and Javier here to make sure of that, honey," Jackie said soothingly.

"Alicia, please bring the med kit," she said over her shoulder.

She eased Mr. Benchman's head over to the side, so she could get a look at his injury. She shook her head, hoping Dr. Greenburg wouldn't blame her for not intervening earlier. His scalp was bleeding and a gash was left behind, but it didn't appear too serious. She made a note to have him checked out by the infirmary doctor in the morning, but he didn't require any stitches so she carefully bandaged the wound and shifted his head back to where he could stare up at a ceiling he could never make out.

Cameron and Javier cleaned the blood from the wall before exiting his room, leaving him to tremble with each roll of thunder outside and ramble himself to sleep.

"She's still singing... *The Wayfaring Stranger*," he whispered as his eyes lulled shut. "Better stop her before she opens the door."

CHAPTER THREE
14

"He's been sayin' some scary shit lately. He wasn't quite so loony before," Cameron spoke as he and Javier walked to the elevator.

"His mind is in turmoil. Many things can push a sensitive person over the line," Javier said.

"Don't start with that psychic bullshit again. These people have mental problems, brain injuries, chemical imbalances, nothing else," Cameron said.

"I never said all of them were psychic, I said some of them are sensitive, they can feel vibrations..."

"Are you the lunatic whisperer?" Cameron teased. "You told me before all that shit about vibrations from other worlds. Do yourself a favor and don't let Dr. Greenburg hear you say nonsense like that or you'll find yourself in the room next to Martin."

"It's not bullshit. A lot of different cultures believe this stuff," Javier said.

"Third world shamans don't count, Javier. They have no idea how true medicine works. All they know are plants and nonsense."

"It's not nonsense. People from all over the world seek out unconventional cures for their ills."

"Unconventional equals unproven, which equals false hope given to desperate people. It's cruel," Cameron said. "Don't get me started on demons trying to communicate with these people either. It's creepy enough around here without thinking that ghosts are tormenting the patients."

"I'm not talking snake-oil salesmen. I'm talking about ancient cures that have been used for centuries... and they have worked. And I never said anything about demons. I said energies. There's a difference."

"There's no proof in that," Cameron argued.

Javier went silent. He could never admit to knowing from personal experience that what he was suggesting was far from bullshit.

A voice screeched from the radio hanging on Cameron's belt. "Can someone please come down to room 13C. We have a little bird down here that won't quit singing and she's keeping the others awake."

Javier knew the room. It was Casey's. He hoped that maybe Cameron would finally see the difference between insane and sensitive.

"She's singing," he said.

"So?" Cameron asked as he quickened his pace towards the elevator.

"Benchman said he heard singing,"

"That doesn't prove shit. He probably has really keen ears. Sometimes when people lose one sense, it is compensated by another."

★ ★ ★ ★

They hesitated before the door of room 13C, listening to Casey sing. It was quickly becoming a labored wailing, her voice shaking as she cried out the lyrics to a song on a constant loop in her mind.

"I know dark clouds will hover o'er me, I know my pathway is rough and steep..."

Javier slid his key into the lock of the door and she fell silent.

"Casey, we're comin' in now," he announced.

Cameron was ready at Javier's side. All that could be heard was the rolling thunder of the storm outside the facility.

"She stopped, maybe she will just stay quiet," Cameron whispered.

"She's in need. We can't just walk away now," Javier said. His palm gripping the door handle tingled with static electricity—a sign only known to him.

He pushed the door open slowly as the electricity blinked out, leaving the back-up generator struggling to operate the lighting. It was dim. She was silhouetted against the window as the storm flashed and danced beyond it.

"Casey," Javier spoke.

She didn't move, but responded in a ragged whisper, "She's in danger."

"Are you ok?" Cameron asked.

"She showed him to me."

"There are no mirrors in here," Cameron said.

"She's in me, always has been," Casey answered.

She turned to face the orderlies. Her face shone beneath the emergency lights powered by the thrumming generator. Casey's face was colorless. Sweat beaded in her hairline and clung to her upper lip.

"Are you feelin' sick?" Javier asked.

She nodded and her eyes snapped shut. Her mouth hung open, Her heavy breathing soared into a pitiful scream as her forehead began to split open. Blood traced its way down her face as new lines appeared. Javier stepped forward but Cameron caught him by the shoulder.

"Did you cut yourself?" Javier asked her.

"She could stab you," Cameron spoke quietly in his partner's ear.

"No. Look." Javier told him.

Casey's skin opened as if being scored by an unseen blade, blood ran down over her closed eyelids.

"He has marked her and so shall I be marked," she spoke.

"What the hell is goin' on?" Cameron said, pulling Javier back out the door, slamming it behind them.

"Is she fuckin' possessed?" he asked.

"No, but she's in a lot of trouble," Javier answered solemnly.

✳ ✳ ✳ ✳

Celia ran the tip of her finger between the shackle around her ankle and her skin. The blisters were

33

weeping, leaving raw, open spots in her flesh. Her arm was swollen and it ached. She was sure that the bone was broken or fractured, but the torment she found herself in was far worse. Her stomach churned, full of acid and empty of food. It hadn't been filled in days... not since her last meal. Shame filled her each time her guts complained. She never wanted to eat again after what she had to do. She would rather starve than partake of the stranger's repasts again.

"Be thankful you're alive," The old woman spoke.

"This ain't livin'. It's only surviving."

That stubborn reply reminded her of her response to her own mother, arguing with her when life was much better compared to the splintered church and its shackles. Celia's heart broke as she recalled how she pushed the old woman away. Hate replaced that lonesome longing for her life before when she realized her belongings were gone, along with the tiny jewelry box and the ring her mother had left her when she had passed away.

"Either way, you coulda been the one it happened to... the one that became the sow."

Celia looked to the old woman, face scarred like the other two huddling amongst the ruins of their flesh. She thought that if ghosts could be real, these three women would be called such for they were truly lifeless, chained to the world in a pitiful existence that seemed for all eternity.

It was bright outside. The sun beat against the dusty window pane revealing a multitude of fingerprints smudging the years of grime. How many had tried to break it with their bare hands? How many had never escaped the church in the middle of nowhere?

She looked up to the ceiling, its rickety beams adorned with identification cards, driver's licenses, faded pictures and it reminded her of how many. Celia found herself hoping the roof would just cave in, destroying the macabre sanctuary of her captor and, if she was really lucky, it would become her tomb.

A rumble in the distance sent the women scrambling to cower amongst the decaying pews. All but Celia. She sat just where she was. The engine of that old, black car roared like a hungry animal outside as her eyes rested on those shaking in terror. Defiance burned in her. She refused to give the yellow-toothed bastard what he wanted—fealty through terror. Celia would recede into her own mind, daydream about being somewhere far away from fear and pain, like a child seeking solace in make-believe worlds and people once those in real life turned out to be nothing but monsters.

The sounds of heavy footsteps creaked up the wooden steps outside. She knew it was him. There was no one else it could be. He was followed by the clomping paws of his beast. The hound was as big as a grown man with a hide as black as pitch. Celia could smell its rancid breath as it panted just on the other side of the old wooden wall, like meat that had spoiled in the sun. Dust motes danced in the sunlight lazily as Celia closed her eyes and sang to herself the song she would often hum while wandering the backroads of America, a song about a wayfaring stranger for that's all she was in every town.

Celia flinched as the door swung open. Through her eyelids, she could see the sun invading the darkness inside the church and his shadow passing through its rays. Her song died away and, in seconds, a hot breath spilled over her face. It smelled and felt sickening as it bathed her cheeks. The death machine stood over her, awaiting its master's orders. The dog turned away at a high-pitched whistle to go take stock of the old man's other possessions, all chained and obediently sitting together.

"Open your eyes, Fourteen."

She wanted to disobey him, to hold them shut and never curse her vision with the sight of him again, but she wasn't suicidal. Not quite yet.

"Open them or I'll burn 'em shut!"

She could tell by the sound of his voice that he clenched his teeth. She believed his threat too, knowing how he had taken ninety-seven's tongue.

"I sense rebellion in you," he said.

His hand shot out with the speed of a striking serpent to grip her by the jaw. His free hand drew a knife from his belt, the same that always hung there, waiting to spill blood.

"Let your blood remind you of who you belong to. Blood and pain, they never lie."

He brought the tip of the blade down to open the scabbed wound in her forehead. The number fourteen bled freely down into her eyes, its coppery taste, mingled with her own salty tears, met her tongue, reminding her that she was marked and could not leave the stranger's world alive.

* * * *

"We had two head injuries on your shift. Anyone care to explain?" Dr. Greenburg asked, folding his hands in his lap and glaring at them.

Cameron often wanted to tell him how much he resembled Grandpa Munster from the old television show, yet he figured that this was the worst possible time. Jackie sat in silence, looking to Cameron, Javier and Alicia, desperately attempting to formulate an answer that would appease their supervisor.

"Martin was in a very bad state last night. He was agitated and violent. He hurt himself before we had the chance to intervene," Javier spoke.

"And Casey?"

"She was terribly delusionary. I've never seen her so bad. She cut herself," Jackie said.

"With what? She's on the close watch floor," Dr. Greenburg said.

"Possibly her fingernail," Cameron answered.

Dr. Greenburg nodded, "I want to make this clear to all of you. I'm well aware that we are treating people that are known for hurting themselves, but if I think they are able to do so because of a group of neglectful caretakers, then I will be seeking a new team of people to fill those roles."

"Yes, sir." Alicia said as the others nodded.

★ ★ ★ ★

They were in the parking lot before any of them opened their mouth about the meeting. Cameron broke the silence between them.

"What a complete asshole."

"Yeah. He's never pulled an overnighter," Jackie said, shoving a menthol cigarette in her mouth while she searched her purse for a lighter. Cameron obliged her with his own.

"Jackie, we watched those cuts just appear on that girl's forehead." He lit his own cigarette before continuing, "But I sure as hell ain't tellin' him that. He'll think we're as crazy as the rest of them tied to their beds."

Javier stood silent, his mind couldn't erase the memory of Casey's flesh splitting open. Her warning. It felt more like an oath to him than any senseless rambling... she believed what she was saying and so did he.

"We're on again tonight. We can't let anymore shit like this happen," Jackie said, blowing smoke out of both nostrils. Her eyes looked exhausted and worried.

"Can't believe Greenburg is being such a dick. He knows that storms do something to them," Alicia said.

"He never understands that. He's a college boy—all book smarts and no hands-on care experience. He can sit down and do his sessions or whatever, but he's never had shit thrown on him or chunks bitten out of his arm," Jackie said.

"He can kiss my ass," Cameron tossed his cigarette to the asphalt, grabbed Alicia by the hand and said, "We're getting' outta here. See you guys tonight."

"Be careful with that PDA or Greenburg will get you for that next," Jackie warned.

"He can blow me!" Cameron called back over his shoulder as he opened the car door for Alicia.

* * * *

Javier found it hard to sleep during the day. Night shifts always played hell on his internal clock, but he stayed because the job had health benefits that he couldn't find elsewhere.

He stood in the shower of his small apartment, letting the hot water run down his face. It felt cleansing after feeling Casey's sorrow crawl over him. Her words left him sick inside. He could feel that she was one of the few admitted to the facility that weren't like the others. Her illness was brought on by outside forces, her psyche assaulted daily by foreign energies from worlds beyond those that her eyes could see.

He knew how she felt, but to a lesser degree, because he had experienced this before, when he was younger and unfamiliar with the ways of the spirit. His battle to block his sensitivity had led him to street drugs, a path to hell that turned him into the walking dead for six years, until he had been sent home... to be cured

CHAPTER FOUR

THE CROWN AND
THE BLACK HIGHWAY

Betty stood at the front window. Her hand shook as she dared to part the curtains. He was still there. Byron didn't believe in cellular phones. He said he was too old to learn how to use one. She had already tried calling the shop, but Bill had told her Byron was out on a run. She had no idea when he'd be home. It gave her such anxiety to look out the window and see the man in the blue car again.

Betty thought about calling the police, but Byron would throw a conniption. He had already told her there was nothing the law would do. It was a public street and she had no way to prove the man was stalking her, but she knew in her heart that he was.

Byron had left his pistol for her in the top drawer of the bedroom dresser. There had been several times in the past two months when Betty had to restrain herself from grabbing the gun, sticking it through the window of the blue car and telling the driver to get lost and never come back, but that would only get her hauled away by the police.

She found herself praying that she'd hear her husband's old car rumbling as it sped down the block; it always drove the man away. Once, after the stranger left, she walked out to see the sidewalk littered with smoked cigarettes and an empty liquor bottle left behind from his vigil of her home.

She had no idea who the man was, only that when she caught a glimpse of his face, she could see his eyes were like those of a desperate animal—wild and untrustworthy. It frightened her and reminded Betty why her husband would not allow her to leave the house alone. The world was full of psychos just waiting to hurt her. She knew it was true.

Betty gently closed the curtains and went to get her husband's pistol. She would keep it beside her while she finished up fixing Byron's supper. He was always exhausted after a long day at work and she never wanted to keep his empty stomach waiting to be fed.

★ ★ ★ ★

He preached himself into a rabid fury, quoting things that Celia didn't recognize from any bible that she had ever been forced to read. His ramblings made no sense to her, like the ravings of the insane. Only he felt the significance of his words and acted as though *his* gospel was of the utmost importance.

"You were all marked. It was shown to me," He pointed a gnarled fingertip to his forehead. "Before I ever branded you as my own, you were meant to be mine."

His eyes fell on Celia, studying her as she sat stone-faced while the other woman kept their heads bowed.

"This sanctuary was constructed by the hands of specters, consecrated by the blood of the nonbelievers."

His eyes, blue and clouded with age, never left Celia's face. "Are you a believer, fourteen?"

She didn't speak, only stared at him as he paced behind his altar. The rotting corpse of the last woman who defied him hanging there, stripped of most of her flesh.

"You took part in the sacrament, ate of the flesh and drank of the blood of the lamb who died to make a place for you to become my bride."

She was reminded of being forced to eat pieces of the crucified woman hanging on the wall. She had only been known as Seventy-one and had been killed only a few days before Celia found herself trapped in the church in the middle of nowhere. Those cowering beside her accepted their meal and even reminded her that it had kept her alive. She found herself hating them as much as she did the old yellow-toothed bastard standing before them. Terror radiated from them. He basked in it, consumed it until he became drunk on knowing that he was exalted in their eyes, higher than any god from any bible and feared more than any devils in the imagined hells of their childhoods.

"I believe something," she said at last. "I believe that you are a worthless piece of shit."

The old man cleared the space between them in four long strides. He was not at all as feeble as his white hair and deeply wrinkled face proclaimed, though she knew that fact all too well. He gripped her by the throat and drew his knife.

"Ninety-seven once dared to speak the same way and now she don't speak at all."

He slid the knife between her lips until it rested against her teeth. She kept her jaws clenched shut in an effort to keep her tongue from meeting its dirty steel tip.

"Shall I remind you of why she's so silent?"

He pulled the knife out and ran it up her cheek. His face was red. She could feel his hand trembling with rage. If he chose to, he could take out her eye in a single jab. She lowered her gaze, concentrating on his white polo shirt. It had a gold crown embroidered on the pocket. Below it, a company name *Jeskey Antiques*.

"ANSWER ME!" He screamed down into her face.

His spittle fell in stinking drops on her face as the tip of the knife dug into her skin just below her eye. His hound came from its resting place beside of the door, drool hanging from its mouth in thick strings as it growled, the only warning it would ever give.

"Maybe I should feed your eyes to my dog. Teach you a lesson," he threatened.

"No," she whispered. Defeat soured her stomach.

"If you speak to me with insolence again, I promise you'll regret it."

The cuff around her ankle, along with its heavy chain, reminded her that she had nowhere to go. His voice still assaulted her ears, yet it was now muffled as she felt herself growing nauseated. Her chest felt heavy as she struggled to remain conscious. He released her face, but stood hovering over her as her eyes rolled back in their sockets. She felt disconnected from her own body as he dragged her by the wrists up to the splintered altar. The room felt like it was a ship rolling with the waves of a stormy sea. Celia fought to remain alert, shaking her head as he forced her to lay upon the blood-soaked table he used for initiation and slaughter. She wondered to herself if she was dying... She hoped that she was, prayed it was over for her.

Between her eyes, it burned like a smoldering blade was being forced through her skull and into her brain. She thought he was opening the marking on her forehead once more until she heard a voice. A screaming resounded in her own mind. A voice so much like her own cried out, yet her teeth were clenched together until it felt as if they would surely crack. The wailing became that of a newborn child, intensifying the fire that raged in her head.

Her vision went dark. She was consumed by black, unaware that the wanderer stood over her demanding her to open her eyes.

A multitude of possible reasons ran through her mind. Was it starvation? Withdrawal from being cut off from her usual supply of drugs and alcohol? Was she experiencing an extreme flashback from those same chemicals that were dormant in the cells of her body?

It was unlike anything she had ever experienced. It terrified her, and for a moment she thought the old man, the traveler of roads between worlds wielded such power that he truly was a deity of suffering.

Before her stretched a starlit highway. Approaching her was a figure. She moved forward, not even feeling her feet beneath her. She drew near the person, realizing that it was herself, walking with her arms outstretched, desperation in her face.

Celia held her hands out. A stillness enveloped her, and though she felt her heart racing, she could not force herself to move any faster than a slow glide forward. Longing filled her up inside, wanting nothing more than to embrace the vision of herself. The other her stopped suddenly. A voice shook her to the bone as it echoed down the black highway.

A barrage of pain erupted in her face, causing bright red starbursts to take over the vision before her. Her heart ached more than any violent blow being inflicted upon her unconscious self as she awoke to the old stranger pummeling her face with his fists. He rolled her from the altar table where the decaying wooden floor caught her in a bed of splinters and fragmented boards. She was too dizzy and completely disoriented by the sudden trip into her own consciousness to understand his commands.

"Kneel before your god!" He raged.

She got onto her knees, lowering her head, more out of exhaustion than obedience, yet his attack abated. Celia spit out a mouthful of number Seventy-one. The old man had attempted to force feed her once more while she was lost in her own mind. He left them there with his dog standing watch over his brides, cursing about fixing the flooring Celia destroyed in her fall.

* * * *

Casey was left in the infirmary most of the day The numbers in her forehead stung and the skin around them felt tight as scabs began to form. Javier came in the evening to return her to her room. He helped her to her feet and took her by the arm.

"Let's try to have a better night," he said softly.

Casey remained silent, embarrassment turning her stomach into knots. She didn't want to look him in the eyes with the number cut into her face. The doctor never told her what was carved into her head but, as she felt it with her own fingers, the number fourteen repeated in her mind in the voice of an angry man. She couldn't forget the vision shown to her—the man's face, the knife in his hands. Casey knew these were not things from repressed memories but something taking place in the present. She was never a religious person, but she couldn't stop the terror swelling within her that she was being tormented by an evil spirit.

"Do you believe in the devil?' she asked, her voice barely audible.

"Yes, but not in the traditional sense," Javier answered.

Casey stopped for a moment, wincing as she turned to face him and his eyes fell on the bandaged wound left from what had occurred the night before.

"Do you think that I could be being tormented by entities?" she whispered.

Her eyes looked exhausted beneath the white strip of gauze taped over the number fourteen that had been left bleeding in her flesh.

"No," he answered truthfully.

Javier wanted so badly to explain to her that he felt human energies swarming around her, though it seemed impossible. He could feel the touch of the dead since his youth. It was frigid like winter winds, but attached to her was hot electricity, the signature of a living being.

Her eyes softened at his answer and she nodded, hopelessness flourishing just behind her pale irises. Javier knew she only wanted an answer—the name of something—anything to fight back against. He could feel the anxiety and fear radiating from her that she was simply going insane, and that she still might if she wasn't shown the truth behind her attacks. He opened his mouth, contemplating how he could explain it to her. Her eyes searched his face, needing an answer. The sound of soft footsteps stopped him from explaining. He held his response, though it pained him to see her disappointment. Jackie came walking down the hallway to greet them, leaving Javier to keep silent.

CHAPTER FIVE

NOWHERE

The walls of her room were off-white, the tile the same. When the door was closed, it felt like being trapped in a shoe box. Casey sat on her bed, feeling her skin tingle. The small hairs on the nape of her neck stood on end. She looked out the window, expecting to see a stormy sky or crackling lightning, yet it was violet with falling night and cloudless. The static electricity brought with it nausea. She put her hand over her stomach hoping whatever medications she had been given her wouldn't result in vomiting.

She brought her fingers up to peel away the tape holding the gauze in place. It took with it a few stray strawberry blond hairs. The sterile pad stuck to the dried blood of her wound. She winced as she pulled it free. The number fourteen was left behind, soaked into the cottony fibers. She wondered the significance of it. Why she would cut that into her own forehead... and with what? Casey remembered laying her wrists open. Even in the haze of too much prescription medication, she could recall it clearly.

It was half a lifetime prior to finding herself trapped in the small white room. She was seventeen years old and depression had been a constant intruder in her life since she was twelve. Sometimes she held it at bay, other times she wrestled with it, but it was always there waiting to consume her again. Like so many who fought the daily battle, she grew exhausted and something in her brain told her it would be so much easier to concede to it and offer her flesh and blood to free her soul for good. The scars on her wrists had diminished, yet never left her. Neither had the cold feeling of her blood leaving her body.

John had saved her life, but he had also cast her aside. Her decision had been shameful to him and had caused a wildfire of rumors. The most important among them had not been confirmed until she was an adult watching the woman she had always believed to be her mother die.

Casey knew that she had not carved the number into her own head, though Dr. Greenburg insisted that she did. She hoped that Javier was correct... that she was not being taken over by angry spirits. It wasn't any comfort to think that those demons were not real because that could only mean that she had inherited whatever malignant disease of the mind that had killed her blood mother... the woman John had told her about... *Annemarie.*

Casey's stomach churned. Acid stung her throat. She weakly pushed herself out of her bed and went to her door. Her mind was assaulted by visions of an old man, violence in his eyes and a golden crown embroidered on his pocket.

"Jackie!" she called, but her voice sounded far away.

Her knees buckled and she sank to the floor. Her mind fixated on a single image for a moment. The feeling of the cold tile against the side of her face ebbed away. The stark brightness of the white room and its fluorescent lighting dimmed until it was absolutely dark.

Casey could see only black for what felt like hours until small pin pricks of light started to shine in the shadows. A wind swept over her face, smelling of damp earth after a rain storm. Something white was moving in the distance, drawing near to her. Casey felt herself gliding along. Her eyes made out what appeared to be a blacktop highway beneath her as the figure before her became apparent. It was herself, hands stretching out, beckoning her forward. Her heart seized. She lifted her hands, waiting to embrace the mirror image of herself.

A silhouette rose in her peripheral vision, tall and black, its arms stretching up to the starlit sky. She turned her head to see a great saguaro cactus. Fear halted her there. She wondered if it was the dangerous man that her other side had shown her, the man with the knife. She could hear the voice of someone raging split through the sky like a roll of thunder. When she turned back, her heart broke, the other her was gone. Casey cried out, reaching her hands forward to the empty night. Her voice was still hollow in her own ears as she wailed. Javier had spoken to her of the journey to finding herself and the happiness within her. She felt that slipping between her fingers. She was crushed when she realized she was awakening again to the white walls of Whispering Creek.

"Shhhhh." Javier hovered over her.

Casey wept uncontrollably as he gripped her shoulder.

"Let the pain out." He whispered.

"I was so close this time," she said once she finally got control of herself. "I could see her walking on a dark highway. The stars were all around us. There was peace between us…" Casey couldn't finish her sentence, she felt abandoned once more.

"What is goin' on with me?" she asked.

"Why am I always seeing myself in danger? Is it a premonition?"

"I can't say for sure but I know someone who can," he answered.

"Help me, Javier. Please."

Javier was the one who had answered her call for help. He had opened the door to find her lying on the floor, shaking and screaming. He had known when he found her that way that he could no longer keep himself from trying to help her. Once he opened his mouth to speak, he knew he was risking his entire life but if he didn't act Casey would certainly end up to be worse than Martin Benchman, beating her head against walls… the energy around her was just too great.

****

The roar of a bored-out engine settled her nerves, like a knight barreling towards her in a coal-black steel steed to frighten away the villain who sat outside watching her shadow as it passed through each room of her house just beyond the windows. Betty raced to the front door to look out the peep hole and, sure enough, the weirdo sped away. She grinned, but her satisfaction was short-lived knowing he would only come back.

Byron came through the door minutes later; he went immediately to the restroom to wash up and Betty stashed his pistol back where it belonged.

"That man was back again today," she spoke through the bathroom door.

"He's probably here visiting one of the neighbors," her husband answered.

"He sits in his car, Byron. Out there on the street, watching our house," Betty said.

"I think you are worried over nothin', honey," he answered after a long pause.

Betty could tell he was in a foul mood by the way he dismissed her and, after living with the man for over thirty years, she knew better than to keep prodding him. "Alright," she said and scurried back into the kitchen.

Byron washed his face and hands; the stink of the decaying corpse inside of the rotting church clung to him. His mind was fixating on someone else. He had warned Allan to stay away and keep his mouth shut, but now it seemed that he hadn't heeded the old man's warning. He toweled his cheeks dry and stared into the mirror, his gaze hard with contemplation... his wives would need something to eat soon and Seventy-one had left his work shirt perfumed with her rancid smell.

He decided that Allan would get an invitation to hear a sermon at his church and never walk back out. It was against the rules of those that wander, but Allan had already broken one of the most important laws of their kind by imposing himself into Byron's real life and threatening to call attention to what went on in his sanctuary in the *other desert*.

* * * *

Javier was thankful that he still had a while before Cameron started his shift. It gave him time to follow through with what had to be done before his overzealous partner was there to stop it.

"Listen to me very closely," he whispered to Casey as he helped her to sit in her bed. "You need to get out of here. I can take you to see someone who can help you."

She nodded, but the look of confusion in her face worried him.

"I know this is all too much. I will explain it as we go along."

Casey sighed, "I just want this to stop."

"It will, but you must fight to make things right."

"I'm ready to fight."

* * * *

The floorboards had been replaced with old pieces of wood from the dilapidated hand rails that were already uselessly laying in the dirt beside the front steps of the church in the desert. Celia went to watch through the window as the old man fired up his car. An orb of light opened before the hood as it rumbled impatiently. A doorway was opening. Beyond it was the real world—the one she had grown up in. The desert she found herself imprisoned in was on some other plane altogether, one where the stranger was both God and the devil.

He stepped on the gas pedal, kicking up dust as he maneuvered through the pulsing gateway. Celia could see the crooked saguaro again, the same one that she had stood beside while thumbing a ride. Hitchhiking had been a necessary danger of her former life as a drifter, but she had never imagined she'd take a ride straight into Hell.

The ball of light swallowed the old black car and soon closed completely, leaving her sick with helpless anger. Her eyes studied the unassuming landscape for a moment, wondering and calculating if she could survive out there once she broke free.

"Where the hell are we?" She asked to anyone who was listening.

"He has called it the *other world* many times, though we don't know for sure," The frail woman with sixty-eight carved into her forehead spoke. "Sometimes he just calls it nowhere—wherever we are—he claims it as his land."

"Any of you know what's beyond the desert?" Celia asked though she knew the answer already.

"No one gets out alive," Eighty-two said. "I told you that, because it's true."

Celia looked to her, "I'd rather die out there than in here."

"My sister said the same thing. He came back carrying only her arm... made us eat it," she answered.

Ninety-seven never approached the three as they talked amongst each other. She only sat in a splintered pew, staring up at the putrid remains of the woman who had been known as Seventy-one.

"Her tongue was cut out for givin' the preacher attitude," Eighty-two nodded her head towards Ninety-seven. "Better watch how you talk."

"How should I talk to him then?" Celia fumed. "Should I shut my mouth and wait to die? Turn out like you?"

They turned their eyes to her, pitiful and tortured yet in them Celia saw a weakness that she wouldn't allow to take over her own spirit.

"Look at you. You're dead already," she trembled, fighting back the urge to cry. "I'm NOT dying this way!"

"What happened to you during his sermon? Did you have a seizure?" Eighty-two asked.

"I saw a highway of stars, and myself walking towards me."

"Yourself?" old Sixty-eight asked.

"My spirit, I guess." Celia answered. "I think it was a sign... tryin' to tell me somethin'"

"What's your plan then?"
"To make it to that highway. Or die tryin'."

CHAPTER SIX
ESCAPE

ackie kept her arms above her head as the girl had instructed. The look of fear on Javier's face broke her heart. She watched as Casey held a pen to the orderly's throat and guided him down the hallway.

She thought how unlucky it was that it was only twenty minutes until the start of Cameron's shift. He would surely have been able to help. The orderly downstairs, Philip, was in poor shape and far too old to try to physically restrain the deranged young woman.

Jackie looked down the alarm button on her desk. She had been told that, if she pushed it, Casey would drive the pen right into the main artery in Javier's throat. She was ashamed to feel worried about what Dr. Greenburg might say after the reprimand she had received for her workers making poor judgement calls twenty-four hours prior, and now one of those same employees was being held hostage by one of the patients that her supervisor had noted in the meeting as being neglected.

The whole situation was a shit-storm. She would be lucky to get to keep her job when it was all said and done. She watched on the security camera as Casey forced Javier out into the parking lot before she brought her shaking hand down to activate the alarm. She hesitated and took a deep breath. The police would be there in minutes to start what was more than likely the end of her employment at the facility.

✶✶✶✶

He found Allan sitting on a park bench beside the man-made lake. Allan sat with his back to the old man. He didn't have to speak. The other wanderer could feel his energy from down the street.

"I wondered how long it would take you to come talk to me."

"You know you have broken the rules, Al," the old man spoke as he brought a can of chewing tobacco from his back pocket.

"So have you," Allan answered, turning his eyes up to Byron.

"We each have our own sanctuaries to do as we please with what we were granted. It's not your business what happens there."

"We are still human, Byron."

"That's where you are all wrong. We are more than human," Byron answered.

Allan heard it in the old man's voice, a feeling of superiority, a dangerous thing to possess when wielding the power to travel between the worlds.

"Do you hurt people in your desert?" Allan asked.

"Why don't you pay me a visit and find out," the old man answered, spitting a thick mouthful of chew out on the ground at Allan's feet.

"Is that an invitation?"

"Damn right it is," Byron answered as he walked back to his car.

Allan could feel the rumble of the engine in his rib cage as the old man pressed the pedal to the floor. Fear struck him like cold needles in his spine.

He contemplated calling a meeting of the other wanderers. Breaking boundaries was strictly prohibited, but since he had been openly invited, they couldn't punish him for going to the church in the other desert.

The young man had been studying the many disappearances on a certain stretch of highway, the victims vanished into thin air. It just so happened to be in the old man's designated territory.

Byron was an elder among their kind, well respected for his power and known for meticulously adhering to the laws—specifically those regarding privacy. It made Allan think of all the serial killers in the real world... how they fit the old man's description perfectly. Allan knew for sure that only one other traveler would even consider his suspicions... someone who hated Allan almost as much as he hated Byron.

✳ ✳ ✳ ✳

Javier drove southward, knowing soon that law enforcement would be looking for anyone driving a car fitting the description of this one. Night would only protect them so much, and by morning the highways would be crawling with patrol cars, searching for the poor orderly who had been abducted by a patient at a mental health facility.

"We're almost there," he spoke over his shoulder.

Casey was laying in the back seat, covering herself with a jacket he left back there in case of rainy weather.

"Where are we going?" she asked.

"My grandmother's house,"

"Aren't you afraid of me... that I'm schizophrenic or possessed?"

"There are many people in this world that are mistaken as such, but really they have a sensitivity to energies that others are numb to."

"How can you tell the difference?"

"Because, it feels differently when I encounter those kinds of people," he answered. "Many people called me crazy at one time and I believed them until my grandmother and her brother showed me how to live with what I am. You will find a way to control this... to find yourself again."

She was silent for a long time before she whispered, "Thank you."

"Don't thank me yet. Not until you get your answers."

****

Alba pulled open the door to see her grandson with another person who was wrapped in a thick coat even though it was summer. She gave Javier a puzzled look, but allowed them inside. He quickly began speaking to her in whispered sentences. Casey recognized that he was speaking in Spanish. The elderly woman had no teeth and her face was deeply wrinkled, yet she fired back with a spirit of someone years younger, even lifting her bony hand once to slap him across the cheek. Javier looked to Casey. She was frightened, but he waved her apprehension away as the old woman beckoned them to follow her deeper into her small house.

"She's always this way," he said, rubbing his cheek.

"Take a seat while I stash the car. Don't worry, she only slaps people that she knows," Javier said, showing Casey to the couch.

Javier wasn't gone long, but it felt like an eternity with the old woman staring at Casey, her gaze invading the young woman, making her stomach twist. The room in which they sat, was dimly lit by a single lamp on a corner table beside Javier's grandmother, its light accentuating how frail and wrinkled she was. Her hooked nose reminded Casey of the stereotypical depictions of witches made popular at Halloween. She was only lacking the green skin. Her companion returned after parking his car in the old woman's garage and locking the door.

"Won't they look for you here?" Casey asked.

"No, actually, the cops won't even know she is my grandmother... she lives in the shadows," he answered. Casey looked to him in confusion, thinking he was referring to her having a lifestyle in the arts of dark magic.

"She's not here legally," he whispered as he took a seat beside Casey. "That's why she doesn't trust you being here."

"Tell her she can trust me. I promise. I won't say anything."

The grandmother nodded.

"Thank you for helping me," Casey said.

She was growing dizzy and nausea was building in her gut. Casey knew when her other self was preparing to communicate, she would speak to her soon.

The grandmother stood and beckoned them to follow her.

"Come," she said.

It was her only attempt at English the entirety of Casey's visit but Javier was there to be an interpreter, and, as Casey came to find out, a guide into the planes of her spirit and mind.

★ ★ ★ ★

Celia was startled awake by a hand gripping her shoulder. Ninety-seven hovered over her with a frantic look in her eyes. She was the youngest of the brides besides Celia. Her dark hair was going silver at the roots and the number carved in her forehead was large and jagged; she had fought hard against the marking.

A low growl raised the hair on Celia's arms. The hound was in a foul mood. It stalked down the center of the church with all the hair along its back on end like a black ridge. Ninety-seven helped Celia to her feet and they scrambled up onto the seat of the closest pew. She looked across the room to see the other two women doing the same thing. Sixty-eight held her finger to her lips, signaling to remain silent.

Celia felt dizzy, her body weakened from the episodes she had been plagued with since entering the church. Her spirit was crying to break free of the old stranger and the bloody sanctuary he used to hide the devil beneath his skin.

The dog began to bark at the window. The night was black beyond it. A screeching answered the hound's warning.

Ninety-seven held onto Celia, trembling as Celia kept her gaze fixed on the view outside. Something raked against the thin wooden wall sending the dog into a frenzy of violent growling and gnashing teeth. Celia looked to Sixty-eight. She was cradling Eighty-two, her eyes wide. She just kept shaking her head and putting her finger to her lips.

A scraping at the windowpane caused Ninety-seven to cling to Celia, making her turn in curious horror to see what would possibly frighten a dog who had been raised on eating human flesh.

CHAPTER SEVEN
SPIRIT VINE

Two yellow orbs hovered there, and a misshapen head blocked out the light of the moon hanging over the other desert. Around the orbs, she could make out a dark, vaguely human face. As her eyes focused, the being shrieked—a high-pitched wail of something ravenous. Its face twisted into a malevolent smile, revealing a maw of yellow fangs. Holding her gaze, it brought a bony hand up to scratch its nails against the window.

The dog retreated beneath the nearest bench, its tail tucked between its legs. It kept its teeth bared, but stopped its growling and barking. Ninety-seven put her hand over Celia's mouth, and they held their breath as the creature just beyond the thin barrier stared hungrily in at them. Shrieks echoed out beyond the other walls of the church, dark faces came to peer in at the tortured women inside.

* * * *

Javier motioned for Casey to sit beside him on the grass in the backyard. She was exhausted. The night was now winding down and the horizon was violet with approaching dawn. The old woman spoke in Spanish and Javier translated to Casey who didn't understand any of it, even in English.

"She says you are only half of a soul. That is why your life has been nothing but unhappiness ever since your birth."

"She can see that just by looking at me?"

Casey was dressed in the thin hospital-provided pants and smock. They reminded her of scrubs that the nurses wore, only thinner and in a light beige color. Her feet were covered only in socks. She couldn't argue with the old woman's assessment.

"She can feel it," he answered.

"How will I ever get better if I was born this way?" Casey asked.

"She has seen others like you. You are very rare in this world. She wants to help you find the highway of stars."

Grandmother continued to ramble while she made her way into her house, speaking through an open window to the kitchen.

"You have to find the half that you lost," Javier said.

"How will I do that?"

"She has a way," he answered. "I will travel with you."

"Where are we going?"

Javier hesitated for a moment then brought his finger up and placed it on her forehead. The wound there stung at his touch. Casey understood, but it frightened her.

"You won't be alone," he reassured her. "My grandmother is a shaman of sorts, experienced with things people like Dr. Greenburg could never comprehend."

Casey could smell something coming from the open kitchen window. It smelled foul, like a smoldering refuse fire.

"We are going to find that highway in the stars. Your other self is there. That's where you will finally feel whole."

"Did you have it as bad as me?" she asked.

"You told me that you had to be shown how to live with what you really are."

"You are much more sensitive than I am, but I subdued mine with drug addiction. I had two battles to fight, but in the end, I gained control of myself."

"How?" Casey asked, but something within her told her it had something to do with the vile smell coming from the kitchen.

"*Ayahuasca*, the spirit vine," he answered.

* * * *

Allan felt him approaching, an energy that rivaled Byron's in ferocity, like a gathering storm, only it was tempered by his calm demeanor. Benjamin Hall stood well over six feet tall. His muscular build and dark skin often earned him sidelong looks from his neighbors. If they truly knew him, as Allan did, they would not be able to thank him enough for his service to them. He strolled up to Allan's car, his face placid yet the energy emanating from him was rife with warning.

"Allan," he spoke.

"Big Ben," Allan replied.

"What brings you here? You know about the boundaries."

"I wouldn't have come all the way up here if I didn't think it was serious. I won't stay long."

Benjamin nodded, assessing the fair-haired younger man. He was a coward. Benjamin knew it, but his conclusion had nothing to do with Allan's feeble frame and soft hands... it had everything to do with his heart.

"Need help huntin' them again?" Benjamin asked.

"Not exactly."

A car on the street slowed to nearly a stop, the passengers inside staring out at Benjamin and the blue car he leaned against. They were his neighbors across the street—typical nosy older folks—both looked as though they expected to see Benjamin slinging bags of crack into the window of Allan's car.

"Come inside," Benjamin said, glaring at them as they parked and hurried into their house. "If they only knew the things I've done for them, they wouldn't be lookin' down their noses at me."

He showed his guest to a seat in the kitchen and laughed, "They all probably think I'm a rapper or something."

Ben's home wasn't the largest on the street, yet it was hundred times more luxurious than anything Allan had ever lived in. The neighborhood was tucked into the forests of northern Arizona. It was pricy, but to Benjamin it represented a place he had always dreamed of living in. It was also more than three hours from Allan's territory and over four hours from the old preacher, Byron.

"People! They have no idea," Allan said.

"I think you have forgotten, too." Benjamin's words stung Allan but he knew better than to add any fuel to the fire.

"Why are you here?" Benjamin asked.

"What would you say if I told you one of our own could be a threat to those in the real world?"

"I'd say I need proof, not speculation. One hundred and fifty percent proof."

Allan nodded, "If I show you that proof, what will you do?"

"Same I do to those others," he answered. "Stop playing games with me."

"It's Byron. I've been doing some research..."

"Did that involve goin' into his territory?" Benjamin interrupted.

"Not yet," Allan answered. "But he gave me an invitation."

"Tell me more about your suspicions before I even consider traveling."

"Do you know how many hitchhikers and other people have disappeared on his stretch of highway?"

"Coulda been picked up by truckers... so what?" Benjamin sighed.

"No. They just vanish into thin air, seemingly," Allan said. "Look it up, the authorities are calling him the invisible man."

"Still not enough to go on. We all have our own territories. Been that way forever. It's not our business what goes on there."

"That law doesn't refer to rape or murder. You know that," Allan spoke. "Those missing are mostly women, stretching back into the sixties. How long has Byron been in control of that territory?"

"About that long." Benjamin scratched his chin and ran his massive hand over his face, "What do you think we should do?"

"I'm accepting his invitation. If I don't contact you again, you will have your answer."

"Why are you being so reckless? Tryin' to atone for not being there when I needed you the most?" Benjamin asked.

Allan didn't know how to reply other than looking at his feet, the wounds he left in the past clearly had not healed, they hadn't even begun to scab over.

"I can't change that. If I don't come back, you know where to find me, in the old man's church."

CHAPTER EIGHT
PRISONERS

"Hadn't seen any of them in years," Eighty-two spoke after sitting in silence for hours. The things at the windows had fled as the sun rose over the other desert. The women were rattled and exhausted. Celia felt her hopes of escape were crushed by knowing what dwelled beyond the torturous church.

"He's afraid of them too. I think that's why he don't stay too long out here... something in him draws them to him." Sixty-eight said, carrying over a filthy plastic gallon jug. The preacher had left it there for the women to keep from dying of thirst. Always just enough to wet their tongues, but never enough for a proper bath or anything else. Celia accepted it, only to keep herself strong enough until she got suicidal enough to attempt crossing the desert.

"I told you, no one gets outta here alive. If it ain't him that gets you, who knows what else is out there?" Eighty-two said.

"This ain't the world we know. Hell, I didn't even get to see the world that you remember," Sixty-eight sighed. "I don't know how or why I've hung on so long.

Years ago, I thought this might be Hell, my punishment for being such a loose young woman but I don't know what to believe anymore."

Ninety-seven took a swig from the jug, then hauled it back to its designated spot in the corner on top of the organ beside the altar. The dog still hid beneath a pew, every once and a while issuing a low growl to remind them that he watched over them.

"When was the last time you saw one of those things?" Celia asked looking out the window at the bright sunlight over the desert.

Sixty-eight looked to Eighty-two who answered, "There have only been a few since my sister was killed. I'm still not sure if it was the old man or those things, but if it was them, he drove her to them."

Celia pointed to Sixty-eight's marking on her forehead. "He's been at this so long."

"I was a rambler," Sixty-eight said. "My name is Marcia. I was raised in California, took to the highway hoping to escape my father and ended up accepting a ride from the preacher. I was alone here for a long time while others were brought here only to be slaughtered. I don't even know why he kept me."

"We were headed out to visit our parents in eighty-two. They lived in New Mexico. Our car left us stranded on the side of the road. We looked around for hours but couldn't find anyone to help. The heat was so terrible we thought we'd die of heat stroke... we weren't that lucky," Eighty-two said. "My name is Elizabeth; my sister's name was Annemarie."

"Ninety-seven came here kickin' and screamin'. She had fire in her, always fought the preacher, much like you," Sixty-eight said. "Until he did that to her."

Celia looked to the muted woman, her eyes filled with grief. She nodded as the oldest among them continued.

"He believes that, in this world—wherever we are— he is God. I can only pray silently to the true lord above that someday he will die and never return."

"Did you learn to play the organ here or in the real world?" Celia asked as her eyes roved over the dusty instrument. The music from it had drawn her towards the old church initially, leading her to hope it was a flop house or drug den.

"I learned on the other side. It used to entertain me while I was alone here but the payment for such a thing was nearly too much to bear." She answered. "I rarely touch it anymore."

Celia shuttered, unwilling to fathom the currency in which Sixty-eight had to exchange for such an item, the old woman's scars were deeper than her flesh, that was for certain. She felt remorseful for the hate she felt towards the women chained beside of her in her first few weeks of being held prisoner, now she knew they did what they had too just to survive.

"He's gettin' old." Eighty-two spoke. "At least he no longer wants us for reasons other than preaching." She cast her eyes to the floor. Beside her filthy shoeless feet were claw marks left deep in the wooden floor.

Celia felt her sadness once more replaced by rage, knowing these women had also suffered his perverted sexual abuse for most of their lives with no one to set them free.

"We can end this if we stand together." Celia said. "We'll kill him and I will go out to find the highway. I found my way in, so I can find my way out. I will go when the sun is out, maybe those things won't come for me."

"How did you find your way in?" Eighty-two asked.

"I followed the music through a thicket of mesquite trees." She answered pointing to the dilapidated church organ beside the bloody altar.

Eighty-two gripped Celia by the shoulder, "My sister said the same thing... that she found her way in. I was offered a ride after we got separated, but I never believed there was a doorway normal folks could use."

"I didn't see any doorway, I just stumbled upon this place." Celia said.

"Maybe they aren't normal," Sixty-eight said. "That's how they slipped through."

"And that's how she can slip back out..." Eighty-two whispered.

* * * *

The grandmother presented her with a thick mug. The smell coming from it turned Casey's stomach. It was reminiscent of vomit, but it had a sickly sweet scent comingled in it.

"Don't smell it. Drink it," Javier instructed. "It will help you unite with the other half of your spirit."

Casey understood why the old woman was making her drink it outside. It was thick and putrid, taking every ounce of her strength to keep it from coming back up. It coated her throat and tongue. Its sickly essence filled her nostrils.

"Do not fight it," he spoke as she handed the emptied cup to him.

Her face went white. Cold sweat beaded on her forehead stinging the number fourteen. Her stomach cramped, bringing tears to her eyes.

"I'm going to be sick," she said, swallowing the *ayahuasca*-tainted saliva invading her mouth.

"I will hold your hair. After it takes hold, just remember that we are here. You are not alone."

Casey didn't have time to respond over the heaving that took over her body. Her stomach emptied and, shakily, she was taken to the softest grass to kneel in. She closed her eyes as all the world seemed to slip away.

"Listen to our voices," he whispered.

★ ★ ★ ★

Byron sat behind his desk at *Jeskey's Antiques* while his brother, Bill, worked the sales floor. He could feel the traveler drawing near. Allan was foolish enough to accept his invitation. He grabbed his car keys and waited for Bill to finish pricing an antique set of china to a customer before pulling him aside.

"I got to make a run," Byron said.

"At this hour? It's almost dark..." Bill began to say but fell silent at the intent look in his brother's eyes.

"Is it something worthwhile?" He asked his twin brother.

"Definitely." Byron answered.

He was a few pounds heavier than Bill, but otherwise they were identical. The Jeskey twins, they were always called. Only Byron had the gift given to him at birth that Bill did not. Of course, his brother knew what he could do but he had never visited the church in the middle of nowhere; he had never seen the tormented souls he kept there. Bill never asked questions. He just priced the things his brother brought back, things he never realized were pilfered from the dead.

Now, Byron meant to take Allan out to the church, take care of his nosy ass, then stop by his stash before then sun in the other world went down... before those things emerged.

"If Betty calls, cover for me."

Byron exited the shop, sensing his way towards Allan's energy. His skin prickled as he approached the blue car parked beside of his own.

"Looks like you want to go for a ride," Byron said, leaning down to talk through the open passenger side window.

"Looks like it," Allan answered.

"Hop in, then," Byron said.

Allan knew the smile on the old man's face was only a mask. Beneath it loomed a violent warning. It was there when their eyes connected Allan could see what

Byron had planned for him. Not the exact manner in which the old man hoped it would unfold, but the sentiment was loud and clear. Allan wondered as he stepped out of his car if Benjamin had taken his suspicions about the old traveler seriously and, even if he had, would he bother lifting a finger for a man that had nearly gotten him killed.

The roads of southern Arizona looked like a rippling black river as the heat left the asphalt. The windows were left rolled down. The wind whipping into the cab of the antique car brought no comfort from the high temperatures. The sun was about to set, meaning they'd hit the other side as it rose. That thought was somewhat comforting to Allan who feared those that emerged in the darkness of the other world.

They sat in silence for a long while, the old man pressing the pedal to the floor and speeding down the rolling highway that he knew by memory. Static in the air told Allan they were approaching the gateway to Byron's territory. He looked over to the white-haired traveler who met his gaze and smiled baring his decaying teeth then spoke one sentence, "Welcome to my world."

Byron hit the headlights, then turned the wheel. The car fishtailed, sending Allan's stomach into his throat before the car corrected. The ferocity of the gate being called open sent a jolt through him. It was clear Byron meant business.

An orb of light, crackling with electricity, hung before the racing car, growing large enough to accommodate it only a second before they sped into it. Allan cried out as they emerged on the other side in the early morning light of dawn.

The gateway snapped shut behind them like a hungry mouth, swallowing them without even bothering to chew. They were on a dusty desert road, barely wide enough to allow the car to drive through a stand of mesquite trees. Byron kept his foot on the pedal, kicking up clouds of powdery dirt. It was only a few minutes before the dilapidated church came into view. The sight of it turned Allan's stomach. He knew in his heart that this was no holy place.

* * * *

The sensation of a cool wind glided over her face. The nausea was forgotten, forced aside by the feeling of being pulled.

"Let it in, don't fight it," Javier's voice spoke calmly from somewhere far away.

The old woman's voice chanted softly, instilling a sense of tranquility in Casey as she was taken over by the spirit vine.

CHAPTER NINE
VISIONS

C asey felt surrounded by warm liquid. Her body rolled like being tossed in rising tides. She found herself confined in a tight space. Every time she attempted to move, she bumped against some slippery barrier enveloping her.

She pushed with both of her hands, forcing the membrane away from her face as the fear of suffocation and drowning started to take hold of her. She couldn't breathe, her eyes stung, and her arms were too weak to burst free, though she clawed at the sack wrapped around her.

A pair of arms wrapped around her waist. A cheek pressed against her naked back. A feeling of calm serenity swept through her. The safety of a womb cradled her and the other behind her. The vision melted away as a lonesome feeling replaced it and the incantation of Javier's grandmother grew louder, drawing Casey back from the edge of despair.

She was now a shadow drifting amidst a storm towards a tall white building. A marquee outside read Stillwater. She felt herself gliding upward and stopped to peer into a window. In the momentary illumination of flashing lightning she could see inside. The room looked familiar, though the scene inside was unknown to her—a young red headed woman in a hospital bed that was fitted with restraints much like those that had once held Casey. A single doctor and an older nurse stood over the terrified mother-to-be, crying out for her to remain calm.

Casey felt the cold rain passing through her, as the birth unfolded in a painful, bloody ordeal. She held her breath. There was significance in that nightmare she played voyeur to. She focused on the girl in the bed, her ribcage rattling with the force of the storm. Her heart nearly ceased beating when she recognized the scar on the young woman's forehead—a number clearly carved into her flesh: *Eighty-two.*

Casey felt sickening pity as the abused woman attempted to grip her bedsheets with a single hand. Her other arm was a pink stump that awkwardly flailed as she hunched her body forward. The nurse urged her on, assuring her she was not in danger, speaking her name aloud. *Annemarie.*

Casey could feel the tension building. Her cries became desperate. Sweat and blood stained her hospital gown and more spilled out onto the bed. The doctor stepped back from between her knees, cutting the umbilical cord and clearing the child's airway.

It screamed.

Casey's skull felt like it would split. Rain and tears flooded her eyes. She watched the young woman lie back as the baby was placed in a cardboard box. Her torment was not over. As a second child emerged from her tormented body, Casey felt great sorrow fill her.

The children were wheeled away and the mother was left exhausted in her blood-stained bed, her breathing no longer laborious as she slipped into the arms of death. The peace that stole over her reminded Casey of watching Catherine die. The revelation of knowing she was not the old woman's blood daughter. It was made clear to her. Casey was given the vision of her blood mother dying giving birth to twins.

She had a sister.

Faint light illuminated the window next door. A thin voice could be heard over the rain and the screams of hungry newborns. Casey peered inside to see the nurse, singing to the twins. She had the face of someone who wore a constant scowl, the softness she displayed seemed foreign, even to herself, as she caressed their heads and prepared bottles to appease them. The stern woman glanced back over her shoulder several times, assuring no one witnessed the display of affection she showed the orphaned children.

The song was the same one that had plagued Casey for weeks, one she heard coming from the lips of a woman she now found out to be her sister... a wayfaring stranger and her true other half.

****

"Well, don't you wanna come inside?" Byron asked.

Allan looked over at the old man, the smile on his face widening with each second. Allan reconsidered his decision.

"It would be rude to refuse," Byron said, his voice taking on a dangerous edge.

Allan stepped from the car, as his feet hit the dry soil an electrical charge ran up both of his legs.

Byron snickered, knowing the younger wanderer sensed the presence of the girl he kept inside, number fourteen.

"Come on in and stay a while," The old man said.

Allan didn't answer. The power within the preacher's sanctuary was something he'd never encountered—the unbalanced energy of one of their own.

The old man shoved him forward. Any semblance of it being a place of peace was gone. They both knew it.

"Go on!"

Allan's eyes were busy scanning the surroundings, seeking any excuse to turn back. He felt the calling of an exit gate not far from him. He fidgeted for a moment, wondering if he could make it there before the old man caught him. The harsh words of Benjamin came back to him accompanied by memories of his past cowardice. His shame was something he could no longer bear. He stepped forward, following Byron up the rickety steps of the church, curious about the young traveler he felt inside.

Byron stepped aside and Allan placed his hand on the door.

"You can feel her, can't you?" Byron asked.

Allan nodded, turning his eyes to the old man. He knew in his heart that the girl was not there of her own free will. The place reeked of blood and death. The hot desert wind carried their scent into Allan's nostrils and left its rancid taste on his tongue. A growl issued from the opposite side of the door. It filled his heart with helpless warning. His gaze went from steely suspicion to terror.

"Guard dog." Byron chuckled. "He won't bite...unless I tell him to."

Allan took a step back, only to bump into the preacher who stepped into his path. Byron gripped Allan by the back of the neck.

"Come on. Don't you wanna see what I've been up to, Mr. Detective?" Byron asked. "Don't you wanna meet my new friend?"

Allan's mouth went dry, his hands felt numb. Byron shoved him violently forward against the door.

"Open it. Now!"

Allan did as he was told. He didn't even have to see the preacher's "wives" chained to the floor, the blood-stained inverted cross where once the bodies of those Byron claimed deserved to be eaten had hung. He covered his eyes to it all before it could register in his mind, but the old man pulled his hands away and made him look, made his eyes take pictures to be stored in his memory, things he could never erase from his mind.

Allan vomited at the taste of decay, at seeing the women like walking corpses cowering in the shadows. The beast of a dog leapt at him, its weight knocked him to the floor. He couldn't catch his breath as he fought to keep its slobbering maw away from his face.

"We have a guest," Byron announced. "Why don't we make him feel at home?"

★ ★ ★ ★

A light filled her eyes, a burning orb of pure heat. Her pale skin felt as if it would blister beneath it. Casey tried to turn her face away from the mass before it left her blind. A breeze blew through her hair; the ball of fire rose into the horizon of a churning sky. She found herself standing on the shoulder of a desert highway. Heat came off the blacktop to be chased away by the wind of an approaching storm.

Thunderheads stacked up high, consuming the pale blue in dirty grey. Lightning danced among the clouds and thunder rolled down the road to greet her. A second roar from behind her rivaled that of the storm before her.

Casey turned to see something black hurtling towards her, a beast of steel, its driver grinning a yellow-toothed grin. Her heart stuttered because she knew death rode with him. The old woman's voice invaded the surroundings, echoing across the desert, calling Casey back home.

Javier hovered over Casey, watching her eyelids flutter. The *ayahuasca* had taken hold of her quickly. It was better that way. Some people were ravaged by nausea but never got to see the things their soul was hiding. He just prayed that she would be granted the sight of those things keeping her spirit divided. It was only then that her torment would end.

****

Benjamin was on his back porch. A cloud of cigar smoke hung around him as he sat in contemplation. His laptop sat in his lap. He typed in the sinister moniker that Allan had accused Byron of being—*the invisible man.* It took a few moments until he located a site dedicated to unsolved mysteries.

Under the state of Arizona, he found a few reference points to supernatural mysteries. It named a sasquatch creature. Benjamin wasn't surprised to see it listed because he knew it existed. It too could travel between worlds and so kept from being hunted down by angry mobs of humans.

The site also warned of Navajo skinwalkers, Benjamin knew too well that they were also real but weren't born travelers; they achieved it through the drinking of powerful herbs. They adorned themselves in animal skins and roamed the dimensions, seeking only to do evil... Benjamin had killed a few.

It listed eyewitness accounts of aliens and ghosts. Neither shocked him in the least. They were drawn to the earth's energy. Then, finally, he found what he sought. His heart, for a moment, had hoped that Allan was full of shit, but it was there in old newspaper clippings and missing persons reports. One stated that an entire busload of missionaries had been abducted on the way to Mexico. they had been going to build churches for the less fortunate.

His skin rose into gooseflesh. The authorities denied the existence of a serial killer and instead blamed it on a handful of ramblers and truckers who frequented the lonesome stretch of road. They had no evidence to go on, only people who had never made it to their destinations.

He couldn't deny how useless Allan had been in the past—nearly getting Benjamin killed—but the veteran traveler didn't have it in him to abandon Allan, even though he probably deserved it.

He stepped into his house through the back door and grabbed a backpack out of the coat closet. He had a long drive ahead of him, which meant hours of buried memories plaguing his mind. Once he dug them all up Allan would be lucky if he stepped into the old man's territory at all.

* * * *

Casey awoke to being rolled onto her side. A mouthful of bile ran from her cheek.

"You are okay," Javier said.

The morning sun hung over her. She had been lost in the spirit vine for many hours and felt weak and extremely sick.

"*Ayúdame*," Javier said to the grandmother.

They eased Casey into a sitting position, then Javier helped her up onto her trembling legs to carry her inside the house. He laid her down on the couch and left her there for a moment to retrieve a pen and some paper.

"Describe it," Javier said.

"I was shown who I really am," Casey whispered, then began to recount the trip inside of her mind and spirit.

* * * *

Casey was allowed to sleep a few hours until the old woman shook her awake. The grandmother threw a towel around her neck and dyed her hair a dark brown color. She spoke to Casey, but she didn't understand it completely, so Javier translated.

"She said she's sorry. It's the hair color of an old woman, but it's all she had to help keep your identity a secret."

"Thank you," Casey said.

The scent of the dye was obnoxious, souring her empty stomach. The thirty minutes it took to be finished was close to torture. Javier had his back to them as the grandmother combed the tangles from her newly darkened hair. He was busy looking for any leads from Casey's vision. He used his cousin's smart phone, leaving his turned off after racking up twenty missed calls by concerned friends and coworkers. He looked at his watch. His cousin would be home in an hour and he wanted to be long gone by then.

"We're headed to southern Arizona," Javier spoke. "You mentioned Stillwater. It was an asylum. It's been shut down for years but it's worth a look."

The news had reported his abduction, a description of his car, and displayed his picture. He hoped the highway wouldn't be closed. His grandmother handed over the keys to her station wagon. It was useless to her now that Javier's cousin, Sylvia, cared for the old woman.

He felt a duty to guide Casey to the truth as the shaman many years before had done so for him, saving his life from the torment of addiction and schooling him in the mysteries of the ancient energies still alive in the modern world. He would do the same for the frightened girl, even if it killed him.

The old woman gathered supplies for their journey while Javier helped Casey into the car. Holding him by the wrist, his grandmother kissed his cheek as he leaned in for her to whisper into his ear, then sent him on his way. Casey watched the exchange, then fell asleep in the passenger seat before they even got out of the driveway.

****

The dog's mouth was so close to taking his jaw off that Allan's face became covered in a thick web of stringy slobber. He felt something roughly clamped around his ankle before Byron called the hound back.

"You ain't dyin' that easily," he laughed as Allan trembled and pushed himself away from the dog, only to feel himself tethered by a heavy chain.

"You can't do this," Allan protested.

"Why not?" Byron asked.

"We have laws..."

"Does it look like I'm worried about those?" The old preacher asked.

Allan took a good look at his situation. The hollow faced women who hid on the opposite side of the church. The taint of death all around him. The massive beast with a black hide and powerful jaws just waiting for the signal to rip him apart.

"You're in my realm now. You live by my laws, and you die by them too."

"The others, the shadows, they will be drawn here like a magnet to our energy, by you and me," he paused to look over at Celia who sat in a pew refusing to cower, "...and hers."

"Let them come," Byron said. "Are you afraid you might actually have to face one this time?" His old face split into a mocking grin, his crowded yellow teeth making it more sinister. "It would serve you right."

He went to the church door. "I only wish they woulda killed Benjamin while you hid, that way you coulda heard them eating his heart out of his chest... pity that didn't happen."

Byron looked at his wrist watch, remembering that he promised to bring something worthwhile back to his brother, and that Betty would be waiting for him with dinner on the table.

"Maybe tonight, you'll pay for leaving him to die," Byron said.

He left the church while Allan struggled against the chain around his ankle, like a mouse caught in a trap.

* * * *

Benjamin sped down the highway, taking the twists and turns without so much as a tap of his brake pedal. He had traveled those black roadways so many times that he could do it with his eyes closed. He cast his senses out wide. It was empty out there. Not another traveler, gifted or not, on that highway. He let his mind mull over the reasons Allan had decided to step into a potentially dangerous situation. Benjamin could only guess that Allan was feeling the weight of his guilt and cowardice. He had left Benjamin to fight off an entire horde of the shadow people. Benjamin bore scars on his chest to remind him of his old friend's betrayal. Did his regret run so deeply he was willing to confront someone who he thought was a serial killer? He questioned if he should even care at all, but the accounts of so many innocents that vanished on that highway was something he couldn't ignore.

"Tryin' to play cowboy, Allan? You ain't got it in you, you're just lucky that I do," he spoke out loud.

Allan and Byron had never seen eye to eye. They'd always had a pissing contest that Benjamin found irritating, but his disdain for the old man ran deep, coming from the preacher's obvious shock that someone of color could be born with such a gift. He intended to show the old man he was born with more talents than stepping through doorways. He was also a skillful hunter and wasn't shy to put evil in a grave. Benjamin just hoped Allan was strong enough to hold on this time. He knew that once Allan passed into the preacher's territory he wouldn't be allowed to run back out with his tail between his legs.

"Shoulda never let him go alone." It was a sentence Benjamin repeated to himself as he sped along.

* * * *

Byron bypassed the gateway. It was invisible to most, but it called powerfully to those born with the gift of traveling. He drove along a long dirt road stretching for miles through the desert on the other side, paralleling the highway in the real world. Remaining vigilant, he knew that the shadows would be drawn to the power within the church. Some might even be hungry enough to move during the daylight hours. He had fought them on a few occasions. They were strong, voracious hunters seeking the light and energy within the hearts of man, especially those gifted with the power to travel between the different planes.

There were wanderers with heroic souls, like Benjamin, who made it their mission to seek out and destroy the hungry shadows—but not Byron. He let them roam so long as they left him be. He could appreciate their primal need to kill, but he wouldn't hesitate to dispatch them when they intruded on his sanctuary. It was the only place he could hide the truth about himself. It was something even his wife and twin brother never knew about.

It was a violence born into him.

He often wondered if he hadn't been given every ounce of depravity in the womb, causing his brother to be born the gentlest soul to walk the face of the earth. Byron had stopped trying to fight his impulses when he was just a young man. The release he experienced was something to which no drug or orgasm could ever compare.

He had also hidden his urges from those who had shown him the way of the traveler. The older men who had felt the power to wander within Byron had never known that he would use his territory to play out his bloody fantasies... but they were all dead and gone now, and Byron refused to let a young wanderer like Allan ruin his true home, there amongst the blood and decay.

Being gifted would never make a man immortal, but Byron had always relished the feeling of getting to live two lives: one of an honest, hardworking man, the other a taker of lives and a punisher of those who were no more than the trash of humanity.

Travelers grew old and died like any other man. It was that thought that kept him killing well into his sixties. He would go out completely fulfilled in any world he stepped foot in.

He turned down a sandy, rutted wash. The car bounced as it crawled over smooth, flat stones the size of a child. It was completely impassable during heavy rain storms, but the clear, blue sky kept him confident that he could procure what he had come for and get back out without a problem.

Byron cursed himself—as he had many other times—for not keeping a truck in his territory. That way his old car wouldn't get beat up driving down these dusty desert roads, but he found with each opportunity he couldn't give up the old black car.

He exited the wash and drove up the other side of the embankment onto a small rise. Stopping atop the slope, he looked down into the small valley below. It was filled with dust covered cars and trucks in the center of which was a single yellow school bus. The sight of its rusted paint and broken windows stirred something within him, nostalgia for his younger days when his ultimate power had run free on both sides of the divide between the worlds.

His mortality became more apparent now as he looked down on his past conquests, his ultimate one gathering cobwebs among its empty seats. He recalled how powerful his hands had once looked gripping the steering wheel of his prized possession. Now they were spotted with age and trembled slightly at the power of the engine beneath the shining hood.

Byron never brought back all his loot. He kept most of it stashed here as a retirement plan of sorts. He had rings, watches, expensive sets of tools—all spoils of killing and raiding the cars and trucks of people moving between states and workers on their way to new sites.

On ordinary days in the real world, he did go on runs for his brother to collect antique furniture, porcelain dolls and sets of fine china, but the need to feel blood on his hands was something he could never ignore for long. His hoard in the desert valley assured him that he would have something to bring back to account for his time away. He even brought back baubles and trinkets to his wife, Betty. Most recently, he had taken number fourteen's ring with the canary-yellow diamond and gifted it to her as an anniversary present.

His shelves were filled with tinker toys of children now buried in the desert on the other side. His wife's closet sported a few coats from women who were long dead, slain by his own hands. These things kept Betty content and gave him wild fantasies of his days in the other desert, eliciting feelings of bloodlust and the need to return. He knew those sentiments were dangerous. The hungry shadows were once like him, travelers on the edge of losing themselves completely to the call of other dimensions, those with filthy souls seeking only destruction.

* * * *

Byron drove down the hillside, creeping along like a black, steel wolf. He came to a stop among the broken-down cars with bloodstained seats and shattered windows.

He took a look around, making sure none of the shadows were breathing. At sixty-five years old, he still had the strength to defend himself, yet he was no fool when it came to the animalistic attacks of the corrupted ones. If they could overpower Benjamin, a man much younger and built like a grizzly bear, they could surely get the best of the old wanderer.

Byron took no chances. He flipped open his glove box on the dash of the car and grabbed the pistol he kept there. He stepped out of the car and quickly made his way to the bus on flattened tires. He slid the door open and stepped inside, where he was met by stifling heat and dust in the air. Suitcases were stacked up in the seats, filled with the trophies of those who had come to visit the church in the middle of nowhere.

The men, women and children, he remembered them all... the desperation in their eyes... the way their blood tasted. It stirred something in his groin. He grinned, strolling down the aisle. Running his fingertip over each suitcase, a sense of triumphant victory filled him with memories of his greatest conquest—something only a young hunter could have pulled off.

CHAPTER TEN
1966

"This is especially true of those who follow the corrupt desire of the flesh and despise authority. Bold and arrogant, they are not afraid to heap abuse on celestial beings."

-2 Peter 2:10

Byron laughed as she dragged herself through the sand.

"Hot enough for ya?" he asked.

Her arms trembled as she fought to keep away from him. Blood ran into red trails behind her. The backs of her ankles yawned open like toothless mouths. He had cut the tendons there to keep her from running away, never guessing she had so much fight left in after the previous night, but she wouldn't give up. The girl halted when stray pieces of cholla cactus got caught up in her sun dress.

"I bet that hurts," Byron said.

He carefully picked up a piece of the cactus and dangled it over the back of her head. He let it fall, laughing as it got tangled in her blood-drenched blond hair. She reached back in an effort to pull it free, only to get it lodged in her shaking fingers.

He looked up at the sun overhead, sweat running down his back and forehead. He was growing bored with the game he was playing and the heat was making it lose its fun. Byron pulled the knife from his belt, then stood over her, grabbing her by the hair and taking care not to get any cholla in his hand. She screamed as he cut her throat. The blood pooled around her face as he laid her head down in it.

He didn't worry much about hiding the corpse. They were in the other world, the one he had discovered he could step into when he was only eleven years old. It had always been easy for him, but for others it was not so simple. He thought about the travelers he had recently met, how they needed training to walk through the gateways, but to Byron, it was as natural as blinking his eyes.

He was in his territory now. It had been granted to him with the guarantee that no other wanderers would step foot there without an invitation from him, all in exchange for keeping the dark ones from reaching the doorway into the human world.

He found very few of the creatures there. Those he did find were feral stragglers, easily subdued and killed. Of course, ending their existence had never bothered him. It was like putting down sickly dogs to him. A simple shot to the head... a swift series of knife wounds... a few he even ran down with his car. It was entertaining, but it could never compare to the thrill of taking a human life.

Not by a long shot.

****

The bus sat on the side of the highway. The sight of it, crippled by a blown tire, kick-started the blood lust in the exhausted hunter. A group stood in the dust and heat, fanning themselves with their hands and newspapers.

Byron smiled, then sped towards them, he glanced up into the rearview mirror making sure to slip on the mask of a helpful young man.

"Howdy. Do you need some help?" he hollered out the car window.

"And the Lord provides!" an older gentleman praised. "My name is Reverend Jim Larson. We would sure appreciate you givin' us a hand."

"Yes, sir!" Byron answered, then pulled ahead of the bus to park.

****

Reverend Jim felt the barrel of a gun pressed against his temple. The young man holding it there had the eyes of the Devil—absolutely remorseless. Byron had dropped the helpful passerby act as soon as the tire was fixed and had wasted no time in claiming the busload of missionaries as his next trophy.

"Drive, old man," he instructed and the Reverend obeyed.

"You can have anything you want. Just don't hurt anyone."

"I said drive!"

Byron kept the gun against the preacher's head while he eyed the terrified passengers. Their fear was palpable, body, sweat and tears. Young men and women, some barely out of childhood, their eyes wide, their minds praying to God that the man with the gun would let them live.

Their prayers went unanswered.

❋❋❋❋

"Your reckoning will come. The wicked shall be punished by the Lord almighty. You shall find yourself in a land of brimstone, eternally feeling the heat of Hell's fire," Reverend Larson said.

His skin was blistered and split, his voice hollow in his parched mouth. Jim Larson cursed Byron daily, hoping that righteous vengeance would be something he would live to see, but somewhere in his heart he knew it wouldn't be.

"How do you know you ain't already in Hell, Reverend?" Byron asked.

He sat on a newly constructed wooden pew, a woman in his lap, her eyes wide with knowing the horrors of his hands. The scattered corpses of the men who had succumbed to the heat, and a few with bullets in the back of their heads from attempting to escape, were beginning to stink. Byron wasn't concerned with drawing predators in the desert on the other side, the shadows were bothersome, but nothing the young killer couldn't handle. He reigned there supremely as the Lord and the Devil—all in the same skin.

The church was finished. Its hasty construction had taken a few weeks and had claimed the lives of nearly every passenger on the bus. Those left in existence were nailing together wooden benches to be placed inside.

The steeple was already weak. They didn't have the proper equipment or the dedication to make it something to be proud of. It stood a loathsome thing, a carcass of what a true house of worship should be, but it suited Byron nicely. To him, it mirrored himself, made by man yet too distorted and disfigured to be a representation of the image of God.

The workers, chained and staked to the desert ground, teetered on their blistered feet, hoping they would find release, even if that meant a bullet in their brains. The women got the worst of it. Not only were they beaten, but they were also used to fulfill Byron's most deranged sexual fantasies... tear-stained angels that would only find peace in death. The only article of clothing they were allowed to wear was their underwear, leaving their delicate exposed skin to blister beneath the sun.

Byron ran his hand up one young woman's thigh. Her trembling sent a thrill through him. The reverend looked to Byron as his bloodstained hand rested on the girl's panties, his eyes weary. Unspoken truth was shared between them in their gaze. "Please. Leave Patricia alone."

"No," Byron said.

"We built your sanctuary. What more do you want?" The old preacher asked though he knew the answer.

"What good is a church if I don't have anyone to attend?" Byron answered, running his hand beneath the young woman's bloodstained underwear.

"You intend to keep us?"

"Not all of you," Byron answered, lifting a pistol to Patricia's temple.

Reverend Larson didn't move, just watched as a blast sent fragments of her brain and skull out in a haze of red against blinding sun above. He wept, but her soul was free. Patricia's corpse slumped as silence settled over those chained to the burning desert soil. Jim looked to each of them, their faces also begged for the embrace of God. Prayers of death passed through their exhausted minds.

"Get back to work." Byron ordered.

"I want this finished before nightfall... your baptism is tonight."

* * * *

2014

Byron could still remember their cries as he had doused them in gasoline and struck matches over them. His throat had burned with the heat of the corpses consumed with flames and the taste of their exhausted flesh being charred to unrecognizable black piles of soot. He had retrieved a few of the larger bones, and secured them to the rafters of the church. Reverend Jim was reserved for last. He was made to watch the handful of survivors being burnt alive before the young man with the Devil in his eyes came for him.

"I got somethin' special in mind for you, old man," Byron said.

The young man wielded a pistol at all times to keep the group in control, but when it was just him and reverend Larson, he had tucked it away in the back of his pants. He had then knocked the withered old man to the ground with a blow to the nose. Blood had run from Jim's nose. He had lifted his shaking hand, trembling with fear and weakness. His eyes had grown glassy as acceptance had washed over him; he could hear his soul being called home.

Memories of the reverend's thin skin, the age spots on the backs of his hands, made Byron look down at his own once more. He was now the age of that old preacher. No matter if he was born with the gift, it would not stop him from dying like any other man. As much as he fancied himself a god, he was still mortal and wouldn't escape the end.

He shook the thoughts away as he rummaged through the suitcases to locate a few items worth hauling back to the other side. A golden necklace adorned with a small crucifix and a ring that matched were hidden in a dusty jewelry box. Byron remembered taking them off the corpse of Patricia after he blew her brains out. There were times he wished he had kept her around for a while longer... the over eagerness of youth.

He held them up to the sun through the broken bus window. They still glittered even after being locked away in that sweltering, grimy, old bus. He yanked open a purse in the seat to his left. It had an abundance of other items he had confiscated, and he chose two men's watches to accompany the jewelry.

He felt satisfied with his haul.

CHAPTER ELEVEN
DOORWAYS

Byron climbed into the driver's seat of his black beast and drove back up to the top of the hill. In the rear view, the yellow bus looked new again as his mind recalled dragging two heavy pieces of wood around the side of it then nailing them together while the preacher was still laying in the dirt.

"Drag it inside."

Byron remembered how his voice was filled with the hasty need for violence, the kind young killers are plagued with, premature gratification. It was powerfully supreme, but he had learned over the years to delay his need to kill. It made it so much more memorable.

If he had it all to do over again, Byron would have recreated the gory hill of Golgotha, crucifying them all instead of giving them a gasoline fire baptismal. The reverend had understood Byron's intention and had no longer fought his fate. Instead, he had prayed as he dragged the makeshift cross behind him. He had stumbled up the church steps while his executioner cackled like a jackal, Byron's voice becoming that of the scavenger birds perched atop the crucified corpses teetering beneath the eyes of the sun.

Byron's mind now only replayed the soundtrack of agony as he had driven nails into the preacher's palms and through his feet. How reckless he had been then, unaware that the nails would not bear the weight of Reverend Larson for long... only until his flesh was split and he was spilled out onto the church floor.

The screams had reverberated through the endless desert around them, riddled with more anguish than Byron had ever heard since. His most precious memories buried themselves deeply once more as Byron had the old preacher man, half alive and still praying faintly as each shovel-load of dirt had fallen into his face.

Byron drove down the hillside towards the wash, he was content knowing those recollections would never leave him as long as his lungs drew breath. He would savor them until his heart ceased from beating.

* * * *

The hound stood guard beside of the church door, baring its teeth each time Allan dared to look at it. He turned his attention to the women, feeling the hands of time pulling at his gut... the shadows would feel them here. His eyes rested on Celia who sat in a pew away from the other women who cowered and stared over at the new stranger.

"He's never kept a man here long," Sixty-eight spoke.

"How come?" Allan asked as she pointed to the ceiling of the church.

He didn't need an answer after seeing all the weathered pictures, identification cards and random bones.

"Usually eats them," she said. "No one gets outta here alive."

"How'd you end up here?" Allan directed his question at Celia.

"The old bastard drug me in here, same as you. I was hitchhiking out on the highway and wandered up on this church, a Hell separate from the real world. He attacked me and chained me up to the floor."

"You don't know how true those words are," he said.

The battered women looked to Allan. Even Celia cast her cold eyes over to him. Their foreheads were scarred, numbers left in their skin by the knife the old man carried.

"I've been here a long time, longer than you've been born, I suspect. If you know a way out, just say it," Sixty-eight spoke.

"Don't beat around the bush. If you got anything important to say, get on with it," Eighty-two said.

"She can get you out," he pointed to Celia.

Sixty-eight nodded, "We knew there's something different about her. Are you different too?"

"Yes." Allan answered.

"Those things only come when one of you are around after sundown. They came for her... they'll come for you too," Eighty-two said.

"It'll be dark before you ever get out of these chains," said Sixty-eight.

✱✱✱✱

Casey leaned against the window fast asleep, the warning Javier's grandmother had whispered to him was not forgotten. She'd had a glimpse into Casey's mind while she traveled and the old woman had seen death racing across the desert. It was the first time since his recovery that he had seen the old woman so concerned. She usually kept a solemn energy as if she already knew what would happen. That energy always comforted him but he had felt it slip when they were tending to Casey; it rose his hackles.

Javier knew the way to southern Arizona. He'd passed through a few times on his way to Mexico to visit family. One trip had never left him, during a time when death shrouded around him, its hands clinging tightly to his soul seeking to claim it. Casey reminded Javier so much of himself at that time... exhausted from fighting things he didn't understand... feeling like dying might be better than continuing. He had spent so many nights wandering the city, feeling power radiating from complete strangers. His paranoid mind had turned them into frightening beings of darkness hidden among the normal people around him. He had shut it all out by pumping poison into his veins and blinding the third eye in his mind, the seer of things beyond flesh and bone.

✱✱✱✱

May, 1992

Javier awoke to a shrunken shadow blocking out the morning sun that felt determined to burn holes through his eyelids. It was comforting for a moment, but his nagging conscience told him that his time had come. How he wished that it would only stay silent forever.

Before he even opened his bloodshot eyes, he knew the shadow was his grandmother. He could feel her. His clouded mind was so frightened by her presence. She had always frightened him as a child. She looked at him as if he were always guilty.

Javier opened his dry eyes and looked to the old woman, the stern matron of his family. Worry was there, knitted in her brow. It frightened him more than the thoughts of her anger. She leaned over him to wipe the film of vomit from his chin and, from her mind to his, she spoke.

She was taking him home before the one seeking his spirit could steal it away like a hungry dog from his tattered corpse. His grandmother knew death was coming for him, but she wouldn't allow it—not as long as she lived.

He got to his feet and stumbled along the trash-littered street behind her. He knew better than to try to run this time. He was far too weak and it would only make his punishment worse. He could still remember the feeling of her leather belt as it bit into his backside from many years before. She was old, and becoming frail, but she was far stronger than him, especially since he was now a junkie.

Her station wagon was parked crookedly beside the sidewalk. She didn't give a rat's ass about anything other than what she had come for—her grandson.

He didn't say a word as he climbed inside. There was a suitcase resting in the backseat, a sign that he wouldn't be returning to his home among the squatters of the side streets of the city.

Javier paused and looked around before shutting the car door. His shady companions were all gone. He smiled and shook his head. His grandmother had dealt with them before awakening him. Her silence, coupled with the knowledge that she more than likely had threatened to beat his friends to death, confirmed that his intervention had come. His soul screamed. The demons hidden there refused to give up easily... but they had no idea how strong the force they were dealing with was.

****

The trip to the village that the old woman had grown up in nearly killed him. He experienced such withdrawals that he felt as if, at any moment, his heart would cease from beating all together. He vomited out the car window. The world outside moved and lived on as it passed him by, unconcerned if the junkie inside the beat-up car lived or died. His spirit was in limbo then, unwilling to continue in the land of the living, yet too cowardly to die and face its judgement... un alma perdido... a lost soul. When the car came to a stop, he was literally forced to crawl up the side of a hill and down the other side in order to seek his grandmother's brother, the shaman.

****

The old man wore a white shirt, black pants, a pair of leather sandals and a straw cowboy hat, around which an elaborately woven hatband rested. He looked to be much older than Javier's grandmother, but he stood proud and strong, just as she always did. He came to greet them but the meeting was solemn. He embraced his sister and kept his eyes on her grandson. Javier fidgeted under the elderly man's gaze, expecting him to reach out and slap him at any moment.

She whispered into her brother's ear and he nodded. Turning, he motioned to Javier to follow him into the small settlement on the edge of a dense tropical forest. At its center was a great fire ring around which were small huts like the ones Javier had seen in television documentaries about indigenous tribes.

Javier was no stranger to Mexico, but he had never been outside the major cities and towns. This was something he wasn't prepared for. The demons of addiction whispered to him that he needed to make it back to civilization where he would find what he needed to appease them.

He scratched the skin on the back of his neck and opened his mouth to speak. Before he got a sentence out the old man turned and eyed him again, silently watching him, before coming close to Javier and grabbing him by the arm. The old man placed his other hand against Javier's chest, just over his heart. He spoke to Javier in the same unnerving way the old woman did, through his mind. He asked Javier if he wanted to become a corpse, to rot in the sun. If he wanted his flesh picked off his bones by carrion birds and hungry dogs. The old man told him that if he truly wanted to die then he needed to leave that moment, but if he wanted to live, he needed to suffer.

Javier was confused until the old man explained that sometimes living was worse than dying, but in the end, it was worth it. This was a message that had never left Javier, prompting him to choose his profession as a caregiver and to help guide souls back to the world of the living.

His first experience with the spirit vine produced nothing to his clouded mind. Severe nausea followed as if his body was purging itself of the darkness he had filled it with. He vomited for three straight days. All the while, the voice of addiction, like a wailing banshee, assaulted his every waking moment.

The shaman sat over him, wafting the smoke of smoldering herbs over his face. The old man challenged the demons holding him hostage to combat. The winner would claim the body and soul of the withered junkie. The shaman took on an ethereal glow, so intense that Javier had to clench his eyes shut. The heroin addiction in him was no match for the old man. She screamed as she retreated from Javier who was lying in a pool of sweat, praying in his own mind that the old man would be triumphant.

He awoke days later, feeling lighter, his head aching and burning. Placing the tip of her finger between his eyes, His grandmother bid him to awaken. He had no idea what she meant but, in his mind, he felt an immense power flooding him.

The second time, his heart was drawn to the ayahuasca. He was called to the great fire ring where *the shaman handed him a cup, and after partaking of the foul drink he sat before the dancing flames. His body felt buffeted by cold winds. A light electrical current pulsed in his brain.*

Beyond the fire light, he could see the banished spirit of addiction. Like a starving beggar woman, she paced, with sunken eyes and protruding ribs. A hunger that could never be satisfied, endlessly seeking to devour and ravage. The shaman approached the spirit and she shrieked and hissed at him, but refused to challenge the old man. She disappeared into the darkness of the jungle crying out in a ragged voice of defeat.

The shaman, walked over to Javier and sat before him. He took Javier's hand in his, then placed his free hand once more over Javier's heart. The young man could feel an ebbing wave of energy being passed to him—new strength to face any darkness that wished to claim him.

He lifted Javier's arm up before the campfire, in its orange glow Javier had watched as his skin began to writhe. It had frightened him until the shaman spoke in calming tones, reassuring that they were banishing the filth from inside of him. Javier could see the serpents in his veins... how they writhed beneath his skin, striking his heart and soul with their venomous fangs... how they would slowly kill him.

His grandmother had joined them, and both she and her shaman brother had used their energy to draw the parasites out from his flesh. One by one, they tossed them into the fire. The shaman was pleased that Javier—who had the old man's blood running in his veins—had done so admirably, for he had seen many men die at the hands of the hungry woman. He asked a favor then—one that Javier promised to fulfill.

Javier still didn't know how he had lived through it all but he was certain that the strength of his grandmother had something to do with it. She had stood beside him, unwavering each time he had begged to return home. Her small hands were calloused and strong. Many times, they caught him by his hair and dragged him back onto the path to life.

CHAPTER TWELVE
SHADOW HUNTERS

asey's fight was different; it was not chemically induced, but born into her. She had a double soul, a twin who shared the womb, holding her as she developed. Their separation had been something that had torn their souls apart.

Javier was certain that her sister would be just as troubled. In many cultures, it was believed births like that created gifted individuals. He believed it.

Javier could feel it radiating off her the minute she had been brought to Whispering Creek. Something powerful had hung about her, and he refused to let it drive her to insanity as it had done to other poor souls like Martin Benchman—and that old man hadn't had an ounce of the energy about him that Casey had.

She would have been a lost cause in only a few more months, joining those who were broken beyond repair, their minds irretrievable. Javier refused to let Casey become one of them. He now believed that his purpose for surviving the hell he had lived through was to guide others who were lost... even if it took his life.

Casey stirred in her sleep, groggily singing the tune she had wailed before the number had appeared carved in her forehead. He wanted to know its significance, and who the stranger was that wrought the blade that had left it there.

The drive would be nearly thirteen hours. It was early still and he was confident they would reach Tucson, Arizona by nightfall.

* * * *

Benjamin blew into Tucson as evening fell, stopping for gas and a moment to steady himself. The reports of the deeds committed by the invisible man gnawed at him. Those with the gift sometimes grew so corrupted by the power within them that they became a thing of darkness, just one step from the hungry shadows on the other side.

Byron would be on the precipice of that change... if he truly was the hunter stalking those lonesome desert highways. Ben's gut feeling told him Allan was telling the truth.

He dialed his old friend's cell phone number and got a busy signal. Now he knew that Allan was on the other side. He had accepted Byron's invitation like he said he would. Benjamin had hoped that Allan would be too cowardly to step foot in the old man's territory but he had been wrong.

Dusk was racing away towards night; the hunters walking the desert beyond the doorway wouldn't come until the darkness fell there. It gave him a little time.

Allan would find himself caught in a situation much like one he had faced years before when he had abandoned Ben. The traveler's chest felt tight around his scars. Sweat built in his palms. Twenty years in the military defending the real world had taught him to heed his misgivings, and a lifetime as a wanderer had cemented his faith in his sensitivity. All those nights spent waiting for flying bullets, falling bombs, and moving shadows.

Tucson felt that way now. He knew that war was coming.

* * * *

Byron passed into the real world, leaving the evening sun of nowhere behind him, and drove straight into the darkness of the real world. He forced the gas pedal to the floor. It was nearly seven o'clock and Betty would be concerned. Bill would have to wait until the following day to get his hands on the jewelry that Byron had gathered from the bus. He had learned over the years not to question his twin brother, and to just accept the treasures he returned with.

As he passed by the corner store, his skin hummed. He slammed on the brakes, leaving two black streaks on the faded pavement. He sat with his engine roaring, staring over at the gas station. It was empty but for the worker inside, but he knew a traveler was close, he could feel it.

"Benjamin," he snarled.

* * * *

Betty sat across from her husband, drinking a cup of milk and eating a slice of cake. She talked incessantly about her housework, crochet projects and the evening news. She had bought his excuse that he was held up in another county waiting on an item and his drive back had made him miss dinner, a common story he had used over the years.

His mind was on the church in the middle of nowhere. It would be into the early morning hours there. He wondered if any hunters had been drawn during the night to the two inside with the gift.

"I never saw that man today," Betty said.

"He won't be coming back," Byron said. "He won't be bothering you anymore."

"And you're sure of this?" She asked.

"I had a coming to Jesus talk with him," he grinned.

"My hero!" She beamed.

"Always, my Seventy-six!" He winked.

The use of her nickname made her blush. To her, it was a sweet reminder of all the years they had spent together. To him, it was proof that he was still human, that he had the capacity to love something without destroying it. He had married her to appear normal but, over the years, he developed a fondness for her, a loyalty and kindness that he would show no other soul alive.

She was a sweet woman, never loose or flirtatious, modest even in the bedroom. It was those qualities that had kept her alive, though she never knew it. In all her years Betty had never seen a violent outburst from her husband, but he had always carried himself with a silent strength, like a cowboy from a black and white movie. His demeanor was one of the first things she had been attracted to, coupled with his rugged handsomeness. She could still see it after all those years.

She ran her fingertip over the canary-yellow diamond ring he had given her for their anniversary. She cherished it so much. He never failed to surprise her with his tokens of love. She understood a man's need for his own space and never encroached on it. She thought that it was the secret to a great marriage. She had no idea she was nurturing his second life, the one that played out in a world she never imagined could exist.

Betty was busy washing dishes while Byron went to sit in his recliner, reminiscing of his younger days before his body had been ravaged by age. He had been what a lot of women would consider good looking, light brown hair, blue eyes and a boyish smile. He had used that charm to lure many women off the roadsides. None of them had lived to speak of his true character, the one he kept hidden from his wife and brother—the monster within.

His eyes roved past the television to the china cabinet and the shelves above the mantle, all containing the spoils of his past conquests. Some men mounted heads of animals above their fireplaces. How they boasted of their hunts, rife with mortal danger while stalking carnivorous cats and man-eating grizzlies.

Byron chuckled internally at them. It didn't take much, in his eyes, to kill an animal, but to take the life of prey who could beg you to stop? That took true heart... or a lack there of.

"Would you like somethin' to drink?" His wife called from the kitchen.

"No thanks, darlin'," he answered.

His mind returned to the intruder in his territory, Benjamin, thoughts of cutting his heart out vividly playing in Byron's mind.

★★★★

"I know you can feel it," Allan said. "The mounting anxiety inside you."

Celia only nodded.

"It's been there your whole life, right? You just don't know what will ever relieve it?"

He stood to drag his chain along as he drew close to her. "Some try to drown it in drugs and alcohol."

"Get on with it," Eighty-two said impatiently watching the sun falling.

"Pull all of that anxiety. That fear. Pull it together and focus it here," Allan answered, pointing to his forehead.

Celia closed her eyes. It was true. She could feel an overwhelming hum inside of her. Her forehead ached, like it did when she spent too many days away from the bottle. Her gut reaction had been to bury it in mountains of cocaine, but her life had moved on from that destructive stage abruptly after accepting a ride from a stranger in a black car. This bloodstained church had become a forced rehabilitation center, cleaning her veins of arsenic, but filling her soul with hopeless dread.

She opened her eyes to see the faces of the desperate prisoners of the church. Some had spent half of their lives there in the grip of the old preacher, swallowing what water he left them and eating scraps of corpses. The pressure was suffocating her.

"I can't do it," Celia said. "Nothing is happening. I just have a headache."

"Just close your eyes," Allan said.

"Why don't you just take us all out?" She snapped.

"You have to know this is for your own good. Besides, what if I don't live long enough to open the way out?" he asked.

The moon was rising over the desert on the other side of the doorway, casting its long yellow fingers over the tree tops, reaching out to the dilapidated church.

"They will come, or Byron will come back. He will kill me if he gets the chance," Allan said.

"Close your eyes. I don't care how much it hurts. See through that burning eye in the center of your head. Look out the window. Tell me about the door you see."

"It's there?" asked Eighty-two.

"Only we can find it," Allan spoke to Celia. "Focus your mind."

"How? I'm tryin' and nothin' is working."

"Find something that calms you, that's how we all learn," he said.

Allan could feel a presence out in the gathering darkness. It sent a shock through him. He looked back out the closest window just as a shadow flitted between the *palo verde* and *mesquite* trees. He jumped at the sound of Celia's voice as she began to sing "The Wayfaring Stranger", a song that had always twisted his stomach into a lonesome knot.

The dog whined, then hesitantly began to growl, a low rumble in its chest, a warning. It too knew what was out there in the desert making its way stealthily towards the church.

"I want to help her along," Sixty-eight said and rose from her seat.

The blaring of the church organ accompanied Celia as Sixty-eight attempted to give strength to the young woman.

Celia's voice was ragged, her breathing deepening as she matched the lonesome tune of the organ. Allan could feel her energy aligning. The organ startled the hunters back for a moment to hide in the darkness of the trees.

"Don't stop until you feel a fire between your eyes," he whispered.

Her mind went to a place on a starlit highway. Her forehead began to burn as she strode forward. Walking towards her was her other self, arms outstretched. With each step, Celia could feel the flames that Allan had spoken of.

"It will ignite, like striking a match. It will hurt the first time, but don't let go of it."

The girl walking towards her now had dark hair. Her forehead was also scarred with the number fourteen. Celia felt the agony in her skull, but didn't halt. She quickened her steps until she was running straight for the other her. Her brain felt as if it was boiling in her head. When the vision faded, she opened her eyes to a new world around her.

Celia sung haggardly, swaying in her seat.

"Is it working?" Eighty-two asked.

Allan nodded. "Yes. I can feel her change."

Celia went silent as tears streamed down her cheeks, her eyes studied them one by one. Sixty-eight let the organ music fade to silence at a nod from Allan. The frail figures of the other prisoners glowed faintly as if their skin was made of moonlight. Celia looked at Allan. His body pulsed brightly like lightning was dancing over him.

"It's only this bright after dark. Look out the window. Describe it to me," he instructed.

Celia turned weakly to stare out the same window she had been looking out for weeks, daydreaming of other worlds.

"I can see it—a door of green light," she whispered.

"They only glow like that in the dark. During the day, you need to feel for them. It's not that hard... we're drawn to them. That's probably how you ended up here, thinking it was your drifter's intuition, but it was something far greater," Allan said.

"After all this time... I never thought I'd see a day when a way out would actually become reality." Eighty-two said. Her voice broke as she began to cry. She covered her mouth with a shaking hand, as a shrill shrieking echoed through the still night.

Scrambling away from the windows, they were reminded of the chains around their ankles, holding them there captive inside the rotten wooden building.

Celia glanced out the window. The vision of the doorway had become obscured with masses of moving darkness. Eyes glowed in the black shapes. The hunters were gathering to assault the unholy sanctuary.

"What are they doing?" she whispered.

"Many of them will come for us. Some will crowd the doorway, hoping to get to the other side."

"What will they do there?"

"The same they will do here. to us... kill anyone they can overpower," he answered.

CHAPTER THIRTEEN
BENJAMIN

Casey lurched forward, screaming. Her mind was filled with darkness populated with hungry eyes and a feeling of loss. Before she awoke fully, she could see a doorway made of light, and utter blackness consuming it.

"Are you ok?" Javier asked.

"I was seeing through her eyes again," Casey answered.

"What was she trying to tell you?"

"She is in an unholy place... but I could see a doorway... a way out."

"We'll be in Tucson in a few hours," Javier said.

"I don't know if we will make it in time to reach her." Casey said, tears wetting her eyes.

"We will. Just stay strong."

She looked to Javier. He was confident in his answer but she was still so confused. How she would even find her sister? It felt hopeless, like grasping for thin threads only to have them slip between her fingers each time.

* * * *

Creatures of pure darkness gathered about the church, tasting the air with tongues made of shadow. They detected their prey within the dilapidated church. The monstrous shadows rushed to the building to feed, while more of them scrambled from the trees, surrounding the doorway hoping to get through.

The prisoners were shocked by what came crawling out of the shadows. Beings with long, black hands fixed with claws. A swarm of them rushed violently forth, breaking out the old windows on either side.

Terror swept through the room as number Ninety-seven was dragged through a busted window. In the darkness, Celia and Allan could see the black silhouettes of the beasts feeding upon the unlucky woman's heart... as if life hadn't been cruel enough. In an instant, the room was flooded by the biting, clawing creatures of the dark.

"Everyone get together and fight them. Don't get separated!" Allan cried out.

Grouping together, they dragged their chains close to one another. They picked up anything they could to try and beat the creatures away, until soon they were surrounded by the monsters.

Barking and snarling resounded as the large dog fought the shadows. It nipped and bit at the darkness gathering all around. He snarled and slashed with tooth and claw and took two of the creatures down, but their numbers were too great. Before long, a clawed hand swept the massive hound off its feet, and a slash to its gut ended the valiant struggle, leaving the vicious guardian in a pool of gathering blood.

Celia witnessed the battle as she too swung a piece of broken wood from one of the splintered pews. She felt as if the war they now fought would end the same way. There were too many of the terrifying creatures for them to have a chance to win. She wanted to fight and take as many as she could down with her as she wielded her measly weapon.

Back to back now, they were struggling to keep up with the onslaught now, and more of the dark creatures were finding their way into the church. Darkness surrounded them and they could see no end in sight, no way of escape. On they fought, swinging and striking though driving the creatures away seemed impossible now. The room was overtaken by the dark things. Some began creeping along the ceiling in an attempt to drop down on the humans below.

Celia swung and cracked two heads, but had no time to feel accomplished because another of the beasts ran up to fill the gap. It seemed hopeless. Suddenly, a noise resounded from outside of the church. A loud blaring call Celia felt she should recognize from her life in the real world.

In the madness of the moment, they were shocked when a car horn sounded again and, through the sea of shadow, a pair of headlights came crashing. It knocked monsters left and right, plowing a path through to them and stopping just a few feet away. The high beams on the hood seemed to blast holes through the dark monsters. It cut through them, leaving them scrambling for any dark corner to hide in. Some of the monsters fell mortally wounded from the battering ram of a car as others fled back out into the night.

Benjamin swung the car door open, then bashed more of the monsters with a tire iron. Soon, there was a wide opening around the car. Only a few more brazen creatures stood for a moment, slashing the air with their claws and hissing, before exiting out the broken windows.

"What are you waiting for?" he called out to them.

"We're all chained up," Allan answered.

"We'll fix that and then we're gettin' the hell out of here," Benjamin said.

Like some fairy tale of old, the creatures fled from the hero who came bursting through the wall of the church in his automobile, swinging an iron club. The group noticed the landscape lighting up. The sun was rising and with it, all the night creatures ran back to the dark places to hide and wait for the sun to set again.

Benjamin felt relieved that the darkness had retreated, but the struggle was just beginning. He had to free them of their shackles that held them prisoner in the dusty old church. His big dark hands furiously tried to wrench them apart, but his strength was no match for the heavy iron links.

* * * *

Byron hurried through the doors of the antique shop. He brought in a few items from his stash, hoping his brother Bill wouldn't ask too many questions. It was so tiresome coming up with stories about how he found some of the treasure that he came in with, or how he had to haggle with some elderly woman for the last of her jewelry and silverware in another city. Most of the time, Byron knew that his brother would believe him or, in the end, at least not ask for more information.

Bill stood by the counter and didn't hear his brother come through the doors at first. He was busy dividing a box of items he had bought at an auction. When he did finally notice his twin, he was taken aback by how Byron always seemed to sneak up on him.

"You scared the hell out of me!" Bill laughed and gripped his chest.

Byron flashed his yellowing grin and said, "Here's a few things I came across for the shop, Billy."

Bill grinned and thought to himself how lucky his brother was at finding such nice items as usual.

"You've always been the lucky one. You need to buy yourself a lottery ticket."

Byron paced the tile floor, silently ignoring Bill's compliments on the jewelry and watches. Bill knew this would be one of his brother's quick visits, just by how absent minded he seemed. Byron would be gone soon.

Something was dawning on Byron—a tingle on his skin. Something was happening at the church in the desert. He didn't know what yet, but something was going on. He needed to get out of the shop and on the road as quickly as possible.

Bill continued to appraise the haul, simply adding, "Yes, these are very nice. I'm sure they will sell quickly."

Byron barely acknowledged that he had said anything before awkwardly replying, "Yes, yes, that will do. I will talk with you about it later. I have some things to tend to."

He threw his hand up, waved goodbye, and walked quickly out to his car. Bill watched his twin practically jog to his car. It was so strange, but not entirely out of the ordinary, Bill was positive that his brother had a secret to tell, but he never had the guts to ask. Some things were better left unknown.

It seemed like, out of nowhere, his brother would flip a switch. One minute fine, and the next he would be spacy, as if half his mind went somewhere else. He had been that way most of their life, and on the rare occasions that he showed any anger towards his brother, it was the type of rage that Bill was reluctant to incite again.

Bill thought of a story they had been told as children about twins, an old tale that he refused to give credence to most of the time, but on days like this, when his brother up and disappeared, it crept into his mind.

One soul split in two—a dark half and a light. It was said that one of them could see into other worlds, a power that was as corrupting as it was a gift.

Their grandmother would often tell them of such souls. He wondered now if she used the story as a warning. The way she would look at Byron was as if she expected him to confess something to her... his secret perhaps? Why was Bill left out of these surreptitious details about Byron's life? His grandmother had always said that it was possible for one of them to walk into such worlds... if they found the path.

Did she mean Hell?

Why would his brother be the one given such a gift and not Bill? The old woman knew the answer, but her concern was quite clear. Bill would always laugh at her when she spoke that way. He would tease her when she wasn't around. It was better than believing such things were possible, and that his peculiar, quiet brother was the one with the ability to do so. Most of the time he was content to play dumb and look the other way. He would lie to Betty for Byron, though his brother didn't deserve that, and neither did his wife.

It seemed like Bill was being slighted in some way, but as usual he would keep his feelings to himself. He would stay behind in his boring, normal life, with his mouth shut and attempt to sell a few, dusty antiques to vacationers and tourists.

****

Byron, meanwhile, cursed as he pushed the accelerator to the floor. His shaking hands raised a bottle of whiskey to his cracked lips. Benjamin was at the church. He could sense it.

He cursed furiously and punched the dash, begging the car to go faster. The bastard was in *his special place. His territory*. And he would pay.

The old black car fishtailed as he steered it off the road and raced through the portal. His confidence faltered, and he worried if bringing Allan there may destroy everything that he had worked for years to create... if the girl, number fourteen, would be his downfall.

It had been many years since he made such a grievous error—since nineteen eighty-two in fact—when he had cut that young woman's arm off as she slipped into the real world.

The shadow hunters had stopped him from chasing her to the other side long enough for a trucker to discover her. *What a calamity that was.*

He had spent nearly a year in paranoia, hoping that the other wanderers hadn't caught wind of the girl found in his territory. Luck was with him then, but he worried now that it had all dried up. He looked down to the pistol on the seat beside him.

He would kill them all.

✷ ✷ ✷ ✷

Casey and Javier parked out front of Stillwater, weeds jutted up through cracks in the neglected parking lot. Not another car could be seen. The asylum was now abandoned and rundown. This was clear by the state of it. Most of the windows had been shattered and heavy chains held the front doors closed.

She hoped this place could give her the clues she needed to find her birth mother, to know, once and for all, if the visions she had been shown were true, and not just a deep need to explain her mental problems.

Javier patted her shoulder, silently assuring Casey that this was the next step. They checked the building for a way inside. Casey needed to find the records office. Surely there would be information there that could help her understand it all. Javier whistled and motioned for Casey to follow him. She glanced ahead and took note of the closest busted-out window. He made it there first and lifted himself into the opening. Brushing the remaining broken glass from around the opening, he pulled her into the building.

"We need to find anything about a woman named Annemarie... my mother," she whispered.

"We'll find her," Javier said.

Casey and Javier stood there for a moment, taking in the place before flipping on flashlights. In the years of nonuse, it had fallen into disrepair.

Javier thought it looked almost like a horror movie he had once watched, but kept that to himself. Unfortunately, Casey was already thinking the same thing as the beam of her flashlight revealed their surroundings. Wallpaper rolled down the walls to the floor and a loud dripping noise could be heard from somewhere down the hall.

Casey immediately became concerned that any important paperwork could be wet, but she tried not to give up just yet. Javier wanted nothing more than to help her find what she needed, and to get the hell out of this sad old place. Both were unnerved by the amount of vandalism and hoped they wouldn't encounter any of the people responsible.

Discarded trash and burnt spots covered the floor of the abandoned hospital. Signs that others had come here—to live or just to get high—were everywhere. Graffiti was scrawled across the walls. Pentagrams and inverted crosses. It wasn't those satanic symbols that bothered Casey, but rather the feeling of smothering hopelessness that radiated from the cracked walls. As they walked, their feet crunched over shards of glass, used needles, pieces of broken wood and other things that vandals and squatters had left behind. Javier stooped to pick up an envelope that had stuck to the sole of his shoe.

He opened it and nodded, "Everyone here was kept in the dark until they were just let go. What a way to lose a job. No wonder it was just left this way."

"That's terrible," Casey said.

"I felt it as soon as we stepped foot in here. Despair, heartache, anger and loss," Javier said. "When places like this go under, it leaves behind so much."

"Imagine living here," she said and her voice broke as an overwhelming sadness swept through her.

Whispering Creek had been hell, but her mother must have been living an absolute nightmare.

"Let's keep going, find what we need, and get out of here," Javier said, sensing Casey beginning to break down.

CHAPTER FOURTEEN
ANNEMARIE

As they continued to explore the ground floor, Javier wondered if the top floors would be dangerous to traverse since the building was rotting away. Casey rounded a corner and, amid the dirty mess, she saw large set of wooden doors. On the wall, to the right of the doors, was a dusty plaque on which she could barely make out the word *RECORDS*.

Her heart skipped a few beats and she nudged Javier with her elbow, illuminating the plaque with her flashlight to show him. They had reached the doors to hopefully discover the answers she had sought for so long. He nodded his head and hoped to God they would find the information Casey needed.

"Stay alert," he whispered to her.

He felt afraid, dreading that somehow everything would already be lost before they could find what they were seeking in the records room, that someone had burned the files or tossed them in the trash when the hospital had closed.

Javier felt miserable for thinking that, but he knew what this meant to the damaged girl. If she came away empty handed it would crush her. Casey took a few cautious steps and pushed the door open slowly. A thought crossed her mind. It was very likely that all she thought she was experiencing was nothing more than an inherited mental condition.

Maybe she was losing her mind.

Casey hesitated, anxiety gripping her to the point of nausea. Javier put his hand on her back, gently pushing her onward. She needed to know the truth either way.

The records room, much like the rest of the asylum, was like a set from a movie. Everything seemed to have been left in mid-use, as if the people there had vanished in the middle of what they were doing. Partially completed papers had been left on desks with pens laying on top of them. Coffee cups sat on tables with dried, dark residue in the bottoms. Dust had settled over everything in a thick grey blanket.

Casey walked to a filing cabinet that had been left with one drawer hanging open, the top of which was stacked with manila folders. A set of wire-rimmed glasses was perched beside them.

At first, she was hesitant to rummage through the files, as if she was intruding on some diligent nurse's hard work she had intended to finish, but after a few minutes, Casey shook the feeling away from her. A note beneath the feminine eyewear had been left by whomever ran the records room. Casey blew the dust away to read it.

"We're in luck. This note says they were to incinerate all of these files," she said. "But it appears they abandoned that job when they found out they were unemployed."

"Is that luck or fate?" he answered. "Go on, let's start looking."

"I need to know if this is real, or if it's me," Casey whispered to herself and turned back to the filing cabinet.

Javier came over next to her and started pulling the files up looking for Casey's birth mother's name. The pair went through file after file, and name after name, but none of them yielded any information on the woman Casey thought to be her mother.

They went through drawer after drawer, digging through the personal information of patients that had resided there. If they had more time, God knows the secrets they could have uncovered. A place like this would undoubtedly have its share, and Casey was certain Annemarie would be included in them.

Casey could sense something urgently pushing her to move forward and faster. Her heart thudded in her chest. They were close. She could feel it.

Javier moved a tall stack of folders onto a dusty desktop, remembering that Annemarie was the name he was looking for. His fingers bled slightly from a multitude of tiny paper cuts from digging through the aged envelopes and files. His eyes kept scanning and searching. He also felt an energy building, calling to him. They were too close now. The file *had* to be there.

He tossed the unlucky ones aside, shaking his head after each one that wasn't labeled Annemarie.

Desperation swept over them, a sickly feeling knotting their guts. Casey swept a stack of the useless folders to the ground cursing. Javier placed a hand on her shoulder and she took a breath. It seemed to focus her for more hopeful rummaging and they got back to it.

With the filing cabinet nearly empty, Casey wanted to cry. She was beginning to think that there wouldn't be any remaining information about her birth. Javier sensed her emotions fraying. Casey slumped forward and allowed herself to cry a bit while leaning against the nearly empty filing cabinet. She let a few more tears to run down her flushed cheeks and stared at her shoes, trying to come up with an idea of what to do next.

Javier, however, continued to sort through another small group of files. Not wanting her to see how hopeless he was starting to feel as well, he let a few tears escape, but wiped them away quickly so Casey wouldn't see him and think about giving up. They had come all that way, hoping to find any clues related to her mother that could point somewhere. Anywhere. A place that her sister might have been looking for as well, an address to a house that her sister could have visited, anything to that would bring them closer to finding her.

Casey had hoped that they could locate her sister's name, since this was the last place the twins had had physical contact. Maybe something there would provide a clue to where they should journey next...

In the terrible silence, Javier was nearly sent into cardiac arrest when Casey suddenly squealed loudly. Javier jumped in the air where he was standing, as

Casey pulled a file from the bottom of the bottom drawer.

"Here it is!" Casey called out.

She was trembling when she brought it over to show him.

"Oh my god," she kept mumbling.

Her whole body was shaking. In her hand was a faded folder, grimy and dusty, and at the top there was a light scribble of feminine handwriting that spelled out the name *Annemarie*.

Casey sat on the edge of the desk and opened it.

Javier hated to sound doubtful, or to dash her hopes but he had to ask, "Can we be certain?"

She nodded, with tears welling in her eyes. Weeping silently, she held up a faded photo. It was almost impossible to make out for sure, because it was so discolored, but there before their eyes was a woman who bore a striking resemblance to Casey... and the name on the file was certainly the one she had been looking for.

Javier felt tears form in his eyes as well. The spirit vine had led them to a major piece of the puzzle.

Casey pushed back her emotions, and began to look at the only information she had about her birth mother. She was nearly crushed by the condition of the file. It was almost indecipherable with the dust and grime. The pages were torn here and there and most of the information seemed to have been purposefully blacked out. Despite this, Casey still scanned every page very carefully, and then... there it was. A paragraph in the very back of the file on the bottom of the last page. Listed under the heading *Medical/Death*, was a paragraph that survived some of the damage:

Patient Annemarie was pregnant and missing one arm when brought here. She rambled daily of having been kidnapped and abused... Obviously showed signs of severe mental illness as well. She succumbed to blood loss after giving birth to twin girls. The babies were given to separate families. Baby "A" was placed in the home of a goodly religious woman of ordinary means. Baby "B" was placed into the care of a wealthy family who had a biological child as well.

The notes were signed by a nurse named Johnson. Casey nearly dropped to the floor as the voice of the nurse singing to her and her sister filled her mind—the same song her sister had sung through her own body. Casey was shaking uncontrollably. If she hadn't been sitting she would have toppled over onto the filthy floor.

She looked it all over again and again—Annemarie had definitely had twins and she had been plagued with the exact same condition that seemed to be destroying Casey's life now. Annemarie's struggle had ended after she gave birth. It made her daughter wonder if she would lose her life at the end of this journey as well.

Casey had to decipher what to do next with the information she had just discovered. The puzzle pieces were there to be put together. She knew that her visions showing her sister in distress had to be real, that the *ayahuasca* had revealed to her the truth about why, for her whole life, she had felt like half a person.

How could she use it to help her sister?

Casey ran through the visions in her mind, trying desperately to discover where they should turn next. There was no information about Annemarie's family or the address of twin "A"s new home.

Casey vividly recalled seeing an image that stood out—it seemed to be important somehow. During one of the visions that her sister had passed to her, there was something her mind kept recalling—an emblem or insignia of some kind. It gave her chills. Her head swam and she faded, losing consciousness.

Javier tried to pull her up to her feet. Frightened, he shook her, trying to get her to speak.

Casey awoke and shook her head. She called out to him, "No, no... a minute more!"

He still held her by the shoulders, but stopped shaking and pleading with her. Going silent, he waited for her to see what was left in her mind.

Behind her closed eyes, Casey saw an image. It was blurred, so she tried to focus... to make it clearer. After what seemed like an eternity, the image became less blurry. Taking on a soft glow, a symbol finally stood out. From what Casey could make out, it was a crown, below which appeared to be writing—the entire name still a bit blurred.

"Is it a family name?... Something with a J.... Is it Jeskey?" Casey was mumbling now.

Javier made sure to take note and remember what Casey was saying.

"A crown emblem… a family name with a J. It's on a jacket or shirt pocket. It has to do with why she or my sister were trapped… or held prisoner."

For a few more seconds, Casey tried to hold the picture in her mind, but it was leaving her and fading. She repeated to Javier all the things she recalled from her vision. Taking his notes and the file with Annemarie's information, they ran to the car.

Casey and Javier were unsure where to go or what to do next. Recalling a market on the highway not far up the road, Javier figured they would go there and ask around for anyone who might know the crown design or the name Jeskey. Maybe they could be directed to someone else who may know. Casey agreed that it was probably their only option. Feeling tears running down her cheeks, she wiped her face. The urgency was nearly overwhelming her.

Javier could sense her need to hurry. He sped along the road to where he recalled seeing the market. After ten minutes of frantically scanning the highway, they finally saw an old sign pointing north directing them to the Heralds Market and Café.

Pushing their luck, Javier sped faster, hoping no highway patrol cars saw them flying down the desert road. Soon the market came into view.

Casey nervously pointed it out. "THERE!" she cried in a shaky voice, her hand holding onto the door latch to open it as soon as he found parking.

He pulled into the nearest spot and her car door flew open. With the rough sketch that Javier had made from the description of her vision, Casey jogged to the front door, hoping that someone could identify the crown logo.

Javier caught up to her and pushed open the old screen doors of the market. The pair scanned the crowd as they walked in. Javier placed a hand on Casey's elbow, silently trying to calm her and keep her from running about the place.

He whispered, "Don't draw any unwanted attention. We don't need any questions from cops. Just calmly ask for any information we can get without seeming strange. We don't need to waste time with a long conversation."

Casey understood his reasoning. They couldn't explain all of this to the police, and they certainly didn't want to be detained for breaking into the run-down asylum. They would quickly be made, because surely her (their) escape was known by now.

She shook her head to calm her breathing and slowed her steps. They needed information... not an interrogation. They could very easily become targets of the local police and that would only end one way... with her being taken back to the looney bin, and it would probably get the only person who could help her— Javier—fired from his job and maybe worse.

No, she could not lose this opportunity.

Casey slowed and looked at whatever happened to be in front of her. Javier nearly laughed when he saw Casey standing there holding a grapefruit. He understood what she was doing but, in the moment, it was funny to him. He could see her as a spy from an old movie.

Standing next to her, he made small talk about the fruit as she looked around trying to get a feel for who seemed friendly or who seemed like they could help. Obviously, the teenaged boy sweeping the floor would probably not be able to give them any useful information. The kid might be too young to recognize the crown emblem. Perhaps it belonged to something in the area from before his time.

"Not him," Casey whispered to Javier. "Look for someone middle-aged or older. Maybe another worker who could recognize other businesses or organizations in the area."

Javier nodded, then motioned to an older lady behind a counter selling pies. Casey agreed. This lady seemed helpful and friendly. She remembered a loud rumbling from her visions, like a vehicle or maybe something mechanical. Still thinking of how to ask the pie lady, she pretended to inspect an orange and asked Javier, "What should I say to her?"

Seeming to contemplate which lemons he liked best, he whispered, "Tell her we were driving through and you were intrigued by the symbol and wanted to maybe get a photo for a scrap book or something like that."

Casey smiled, pleased with Javier. He had really thought of a good reason to inquire about the crown. Far more on edge than she was showing, she was thankful to have him in her corner. Aside from the crown flashing in her mind, Casey had been having trouble finding the words she needed until he had made the suggestion. Casey nodded her approval and motioned for him to follow her over to the woman.

CHAPTER FIFTEEN
A ROARING ENGINE

Behind the old wooden counter stood a smiling, older lady with greying blond hair. She wore an old-fashioned blue gingham apron. There was a small name tag pinned on the right side with Louise written in pretty cursive handwriting on it. Casey approached Louise smiling. After her time in the asylum, Casey had learned that, if you needed something from someone else, you got farther in most situations if you smiled and acted as friendly as possible. Louise smiled back. She had pretty light blue eyes that made Casey hopeful for some reason. The friendly-faced woman behind the counter waved and asked, "Can I help you, folks?"

Casey and Javier smiled back and made small talk for a few minutes, talking with Louise about the fruit in the market, pie crust recipes and the weather. Javier was impressed. Casey seemed like a sweet young lady on car trip with her family friend. He could tell the type of upbringing she'd had. Casey had definitely been raised with some morals and she showed the proper amount of respect and witty humor that made strangers like her. He was a little relieved that the brash young lady from the asylum was nowhere in sight.

Louise proved to be exactly the help they were looking for. She told them what they needed to hear when Casey asked, "I heard about this place from a friend, but we can't seem to locate it. I would really like to see it."

"That insignia is from an antique shop about twenty minutes down the road."

"An antique shop? I have to go check that out. I bet there will be a ton of wonderful opportunities for pictures there for the scrap book I'm making of our little road trip."

"Thank you, Louise," Javier said.

"No problem. That's what I'm here for," The older woman grinned.

They could hardly contain themselves on the walk back through the parking lot. Another piece to the puzzle was now in place.

★ ★ ★ ★

Casey bit her lips nervously on the way there. Finally, they pulled into the parking lot, but just as they were locking up the car to walk inside, an old man exited the store and jogged over to an older car—a shining black sedan. She felt like staring at hole through him.

Javier grabbed her hand and tried to pull her along. Relenting, she slowly began to follow Javier until a familiar rumbling caught her ear. She stopped, rooted in place, Javier was talking but she couldn't hear the words. Only the rumble of the that bored-out motor filled her head. Casey turned quickly and watched as the car sped off out of the parking lot.

"Let's go!" she screamed, cutting off Javier midsentence.

He stopped and stared.

"That was it—the rumble. That car! That man! We have to keep up with him!" she said.

Javier didn't question Casey. The look on her face said it all. They jumped back into his grandmother's car and sped after him, hoping to not lose sight of the black car.

* * * *

Benjamin worked furiously trying to remove their chains. From the trunk of his car, he pulled out every tool he had. Soon, they realized that only Ben's brute strength and a sledgehammer was doing any kind of real damage to the shackles, but this was taking time, and time was something they all knew they didn't have. Celia and Eighty-two sat against the side wall watching the progress with sinking hearts.

"You look so much like my sister. Annemarie was killed by the old bastard, but I swear you could be her daughter. Your looks and hair color are just like her," she sighed, lost in recollection of happier times. "Even when you stand a certain way it reminds me of Annemarie. Sometimes, I fantasize that she did make it, and she was not torn apart by monsters. It's just comforting somehow to imagine dying an old woman with her beside me." The older woman began to weep.

Celia quietly listened, then told Eighty-two, "If our end comes here—on this side—I will be beside you... but if I die, I will try my best to take that son of a bitch with me." The women held hands for a moment trying to comfort each other and watching in desperation as their rescuer fought to free them.

Benjamin repeatedly swung the sledgehammer down onto the old links in the chain. After a while, a few of the dented links finally crumbled apart, freeing Sixty-eight. They all cheered, then he and Allan took turns beating the rest of the chains until they were all freed of being tethered to the church floor—all but Allan. He was the last one to receive Benjamin's attention.

The women were now able to move around more easily, but they still had shackles around their ankles and lengths of chain dragging along beside them. Cautiously optimistic that they could try to make break for it, their elation seemed short lived when a familiar rumbling caught their attention. The bastard was back and would most certainly kill anyone he could get his hands on.

Benjamin yelled, "Get the hell out of here. Get to the doorway!"

Outside of the church, Byron stepped from his car holding a large revolver and immediately let fly shot after shot into the walls and windows. Smiling a yellow grin when Benjamin came into view, he reloaded his pistol confidently. The dark silhouette of Benjamin stood with his arms stretched over his head using a sledge hammer to free Allan.

Byron whistled so the big man would turn in his direction. He wanted to be looking Benjamin in the eye when he blew him away.

Inside, Benjamin had nearly finished doing all he could to set Allan free. He wished he could've done more, but at least at he'd managed to get them separated enough so they could try and run to the doorway.

Hopefully, Celia could pull it open.

A shot rang out and a bullet tore into his gut. Benjamin knew instantly that he was in trouble. His body quaked as blood ran down his legs. Turning back, he let the hammer fly and the chain broke at last. Allan scrambled across the floor towards a window as a familiar voice spoke from the church doorway, "Big Ben. Welcome to my church, are you enjoying yourself?"

Partially obscured behind a church pew when he froze, Allan looked over to his old friend. Benjamin gripped his stomach and held his hammer at his side. Blood ran out from between his fingers.

"Come on over here and find out, old man," he answered.

"I've been waiting for this," said Byron as he strode forward.

Allan slunk through the window as the preacher raised his pistol. He went falling out onto his head as a gunshot echoed through the desert in the middle of nowhere.

Benjamin cried out.

The old man laughed, "This ain't gonna be quick."

Allan realized that Byron had intentionally shot the hulking traveler in a painful, yet non-lethal part of his body to make him suffer before he died. A thud came from the other side of the wall. Allan hesitated. The tree line was close, just beyond Ninety-seven's corpse. He could make it there quickly, without drawing the old man's attention. Climbing to his feet, he ran as he heard Benjamin screaming behind him.

★ ★ ★ ★

Javier pushed the gas pedal to the floor but the station wagon couldn't keep pace with the black sedan. Its engine roared in the distance as it flew over every dip in the road. They watched it outpace them until it crested a small hill.

In an instant, it was gone.

"Where'd he go?" Casey shouted.

"He was right there!" Javier answered.

A single cloud of dust dissipated in the air at the roadside, but the black car was nowhere to be seen.

"Slow down!" Casey cried.

Javier brought the car to a crawl along the desert highway. "Does this look familiar to you?" he asked.

"Yes."

149

It was too surreal for Casey to see actual scenery from what she thought had been just a dream... A hallucination. The crooked saguaro stood tall just off the blacktop, pointing its arms to the sky. A feeling, like an electrical current, passed through her body.

"She's here somewhere."

Javier pulled off to the side of the highway and gave Casey a moment.

"We have to find her," she said then pushed the car door open.

They walked cautiously towards a copse of twisted mesquite trees. Her skin tingled with an unseen power all around them.

"Can you feel it?" Javier asked.

"Yes."

"This is a place of strong energy," he said. "A crossroads exists here."

Casey looked at him.

"I was taught about them in my time with a shaman. He tested me, but I couldn't pass the barrier between worlds." Javier hesitated before asking, "Are you strong enough to see what lies on the other side?"

She shook her head, "No but I can feel something pulling at me, like a river trying to carry me away."

"Stand your ground until we know what we're dealing with."

"I can hear the roar of his engine, but I can't see his car," she said, shaking her head. "I think he's going to kill her."

"Call out to her. Let her know to stay strong," Javier said.

Casey nodded and closed her eyes. She could not see her sister but a sense of dread filled her. "She's in danger."

"Speak to her in your mind. She will hear you," He said.

Casey concentrated, her mind focused on the vision she had seen of that very highway. She called out the only way she knew how, with the song they shared at birth before they were given to separate families.

CHAPTER SIXTEEN
A FAMILIAR SONG

Celia dragged Sixty-eight by the hand. She was weak, malnourished and unaccustomed to traversing anything but the old, wooden church floor. Eighty-two was right beside them as they ran into the desert outside the church.

Gunshots rang out again, reminding them of the monster behind them. Casey sought another doorway, an exit into the world on the other side. The morning waned into midday as they halted. Casey couldn't sense another doorway anywhere around them.

The heat was beginning to rise. Soon it would be sweltering. Their church prison had been as hot as an oven and reeked constantly of decay. The open desert held a breeze, though it did nothing to stifle the heat. If they became lost in the miles of endless sand and cactus, they would find themselves in a dire situation.

Death closed in.

They needed to make a decision about how they wanted to go if it finally drew its noose about their necks.

"Do you see anything?" Sixty-eight asked just as her determination began to fade.

"Nothing," Casey answered truthfully.

"Let's keep going," Eighty-two said in desperation. "He's gonna find us out here."

Casey knew it was true. Her hopes of finding another way out were diminishing quickly.

"The doorway... we have to go back and get through it," she said.

"He's back there, how will we get by him?" Sixty-eight asked, her voice breaking as she tried to catch her breath.

"Sounds like he's busy."

Another shot ricocheted in the distance.

"He'll kill us too, for sure," Eighty-two said.

"Only if he catches us," Celia said.

The two older women nodded.

"Are you sure you can get us through?" Eighty-two asked.

"I'm sure as hell gonna try."

Celia allowed them a spare minute to collect themselves, to gather the remainder of their strength and bravery. It was all they had left after being held captive most of their lives.

Both women were walking skeletons with bruised skin stretched over their bones. Celia couldn't believe they had survived so long. It could only have been their determination to live keeping them going. She knew they would need every ounce of it to make it back into the other world.

"What will we do?" Sixty-eight asked. "When we cross over?"

"We're gonna start over," Celia assured her.

"How?" the old woman wept. "Look at us."

"If we lived through this, nothin' can stop us," Eighty-two said, coaxing the battered old woman onto her feet.

Sixty-eight nodded and smiled through her tears.

* * * *

Byron stood over Benjamin, the once mighty giant, a military hero who had fought enemy war parties on foreign soil and legions of shadow hunters in this world on the other side.

Benjamin was bleeding out. His life would end here, on the splintered floor of the old man's tainted sanctuary. Byron paused as he drove his thumb into a bullet hole in Benjamin's gut, his eyes falling on his dog lying dead not far away. Rage filled him as he turned back to gaze at Ben's ashen face.

"You brought this on yourself," Benjamin spat.

Byron shoved his thumb deeper into the weeping wound and savored Benjamin's cries for a moment before responding, "Every life ends. You just gotta decide if you're going out with a whimper... or a bang."

The old man lifted his pistol once more and placed it against Ben's temple.

"Beg me to stop," he ordered.

"Fuck, no." Benjamin spat a fat wad of saliva and blood into Byron's expectant face.

"This is gonna be painful. I can promise you that," The preacher said.

He lifted his pistol high above his head and swung it down with all of his strength into Ben's nose, breaking it with an audible crunch. Standing over the other traveler as he fell unconscious, Byron began pistol-whipping his face until his orbital bones were crushed and his eyes were swollen shut. He reloaded his pistol but refused to end it so quickly for the man who trespassed into his territory. Instead he kept wielding the gun like a club until Benjamin's skull was a mess of broken teeth, shattered bones, flesh and blood.

★ ★ ★ ★

The old man would never have guessed who stood behind him, wielding a large, jagged stone. Allan shook, his cowardice screaming for him to run for the doorway that pulsed beyond the old black car while it wasn't guarded, but he couldn't abandon Benjamin.

Not again.

He lifted the rock above his head, then swung it downward against the back of Byron's skull. It connected with a dull thud, leaving the preacher's scalp dangling in a bloody flap.

He pitched forward, tumbling over Benjamin who was barely alive. His bloody pistol skidded a few feet away as the old man tried to regain control of himself after that dizzying blow to the back of his head.

"Ben, get up! I came back for you," Allan yelled.

He could see that Benjamin wouldn't be going anywhere on his own two feet. The blood pooling beneath him made it quite clear to Allan that he returned much too late.

"Ben! Come on!" he begged his companion, though he knew it would do no good.

Byron brought his fingers up to feel fresh blood and the gaping wound left by the jagged stone. He laughed, "A hero made out of a rat. What is this, are you seeking redemption for being so yellow before? Did you forget that God can't hear you here?"

"Shut your mouth! I'll kill you!" Allan threatened.

"You don't know what that means, boy," Byron said as he rose slowly.

"I swear... I will end you. Stay where you are!" Allan cried.

"You don't have it in you to look in a man's eyes and watch him die, and to feel nothin' while it's happening," the old man said. "You have no idea... but I do."

Allan lifted the stone defensively. "Stay back."

"It's gonna take more than that rock to kill a man like me and you know it." Byron stepped forward sending Allan rushing backwards.

Not even bothering with his gun, he ran on numb legs towards Allan. Both travelers screamed as they clashed together.

Allan swung his weapon, connecting with the side of the old man's face. It opened a hole in Byron's cheek but he didn't relent. He tackled Allan. Landing roughly, they broke through the floorboards of the bloodstained church.

The breath was knocked from Allan's lungs beneath the weight of the old man. Splintered wood impaled the flesh of his back. His only weapon fell from his hand. Byron forced Allan down further onto the broken boards with one hand while using the other to batter him in the face. Allan felt the shock inflicted by the preacher's fists. His lip busted, and with the second punch, he felt his front teeth come loose.

Allan moaned as Byron relented, assessing the situation. Seeing that the younger traveler was held in place by the shard of wood piercing his flesh made the old man laugh.

"The little rat finds himself caught in a trap," Byron said, standing and walking slowly over to the sledgehammer lying beside Ben's corpse. "If we had a little more time, I would make this so much more memorable, but this will have to do."

Allan struggled as the old man heaved the metal hammer over his head with a cold grin of victory on his bloodied face.

"Say hello to Benjamin," he winked then let the heavy hammer fall on Allan's head.

The vicious blow shattered the top of Allan's skull. The preacher hadn't the time to admire Allan's eyes as they went dim. He strode back out into the bright desert sun, hellbent on dealing with the women who had abandoned him.

He turned back for a moment, knowing the scene inside would bring him nothing but trouble from the wanderers on the other side if they chose to investigate.

Besides the wall had been demolished when Benjamin had come plowing into it. Though it pained him, his cunning told him that it was time to find a new sanctuary.

Byron reached into the front seat of his old car and retrieved a half-drunk bottle of booze. Pulling a hanky from his pocket, he shoved it down into the bottle, then lit it with a lighter in his pocket. In his mind, he could hear the screams of those who had built the rickety old building as they were burned alive in the baptismal that had christened the unholy sanctuary.

He tossed the bottle inside and watched as hungry flames began to devour his life's work.

****

The women snuck back towards the old church, praying that they wouldn't be spotted in the bright desert sun. The ground was riddled with sharp stones in the hot sand. Their bare feet felt every stray thorn and burr as they slunk low to the ground, but it was far better than braving the night and its hunters.

They were out of breath when they spotted the crooked steeple. A gunshot resounded from inside.

At that very moment, Celia dropped to her knees, the muffled voices of her two companions drowned out by a familiar song coming from a different direction. An engine roared like a hungry beast, but she paid it no attention. The comfort that the tune brought was intoxicating.

She got to her feet and followed it, fear of the preacher ebbing away as she realized that her visions were all becoming reality. Celia ran in the direction of the voice, knowing it would originate from the desolate highway. The other half of her soul was calling her to freedom.

"She's here. She's come to get us out!"

Behind her, the exhausted breathing of the other two prisoners became distant. Their footfalls ceased eventually, but Celia kept moving. Her feet carried her madly through the brush. Thorns dug into her skin leaving bleeding claw marks. Low mesquite branches tore at her already abused skin, but she would not relent. She wasn't even aware of the roaring beast at her back, until it nipped the backs of her legs the, with great speed, sent her flying up and over as the car passed beneath her.

Celia felt the snapping of bones as she was thrown over the hood of the car. The windshield cracked and spider-webbed at the impact of her elbow. It had happened in a few violent seconds.

She opened her eyes to intense pain and the rumble of an engine. Somewhere close, a fire burned and the smoke began to reach her nostrils. A shadow crept across her, blocking the intense rays of the sun. She knew it was him, even before he opened his mouth to speak.

"Where do you think you're goin'?"

Celia didn't answer. He knew damn well where she was going.

"I knew I should have killed you already. The last one like you made it out... missin' an arm, but she still passed through the door. I can't risk that again."

Byron bent down and grabbed Celia under the arms. "The Lord giveth. The Lord taketh away," he said, his sour breath mixing with the scent of the burning church.

"Stop where you are, preacher man!" Eighty-two warned.

He dropped Celia to the ground and turned with a smile on his face. The old woman stood with a rock in her hand, her arm shaking with fear and exhaustion.

CHAPTER SEVENTEEN
RUIN

"**W**hat do you think you're gonna do? Kill me?" Byron laughed and reached for his pistol, but the waist of his pants were empty and he remembered leaving it in the seat of the car.

"Drop it," he said.

"NO!" Eighty-two answered and lifted it up, ready to bean him in the head.

"You just assured yourself a long, painful death. I'm gonna skin you alive!"

Byron wasn't frightened by her threat, just irritated that she wouldn't just obey him like she always had. He took a step forward as she let the stone fly. It connected with his shoulder and he rushed her. Her frail body fell beneath him as he tackled her to the hot sand. He lifted his fist and let it fly. The sound of it impacting her mouth sickened Celia. She got to her knees, then pushed her battered body up onto her feet. Resounding in her mind, the song strengthened her. She stumbled towards the old man as he was busy pummeling Eighty-two in the face.

* * * *

Casey kept her eyes closed and focused her mind on the vision beyond a wavering barrier. It looked like heat dissipating from the surface of blacktop. Reaching her hands out, she couldn't penetrate the veil between the worlds. It was now nighttime in her world but stark daylight on the other side with her sister and her prison—the burning church.

She felt trapped, watching her sister beyond the mesquite trees as she was assaulted by a white-haired man who had run her down with his car. He appeared old, yet his strength was that of someone much younger. He turned on a skeletal wraith of a woman who was trying to defend Casey's twin and began to viciously beat her as well. Casey watched as her twin rose, wobbling as she attempted to rescue the other prisoner of the desert church.

"What can you see?" Javier asked quietly.

"He's going to kill her," she answered.

"No. Send her strength. Sing to her if that is your bond. It can't end this way."

Casey nodded and, with a ragged voice, she sang as tears streamed down her cheeks.

✱ ✱ ✱ ✱

Celia fell onto Byron's back, grabbing a fistful of his hair. He cursed and flung his arm back to knock her away, but she held on. Sinking her teeth into the side of his neck, Celia bit with every last ounce of her strength. He screamed and brought his opposite fist up to punch her in the nose but she still would not relent. Pain meant nothing to her anymore.

He rolled off of Eighty-two, taking Celia with him. Her jaws clenched tighter until blood filled her mouth and a loose chunk of flesh danced over her tongue. Byron's collar was soaked in blood. His face was red with rage as he brought his fist up, ready to beat Celia into oblivion.

A gunshot nearly deafened her. The old man wheezed, his eyes filling with disbelief. He turned to see Sixty-eight standing with his gun in her hand, her arms trembling so hard that she nearly dropped it in the dirt.

"Look what you left in your car," she said.

Celia felt relief washing over her as the fragile woman stood her ground. "You thought you'd just burn us all up in that hellhole."

She pulled the trigger again. A bullet tore through his shoulder, leaving a mist of blood hanging in the arid desert atmosphere. The scent of gunpowder and sweat drifted from the old woman who smiled a toothless grin of satisfaction.

"I got a better plan," she said, feeling the power of holding his existence in her hands. "We're gonna burn your ass instead!"

"If I'm going to Hell, you're all comin' with me." he said. "I promise you that."

* * * *

Casey swayed on her feet. She couldn't hold the vision much longer. She could feel her strength slipping away when the old man fell over, her sister still latched onto his neck like a wild animal in the throes of death. They scrambled in the dirt, his blood running bright red onto his filthy shirt.

When he got the upper hand, Casey nearly blacked out. Death was coming for a sister that she had never gotten the chance to hold or communicate with, other than their frantic mental exchanges. A part of herself was being murdered right in front of her eyes.

She reached out. The electricity of the barrier ran up her arms and she cried out, losing the words to the song that had kept them bound together since birth.

The sound of a gunshot sent a shock through her chest as she wept. An old woman, so thin and haggard that it was a miracle she had the strength to wield a gun, stood in the dirt, bare-footed and half-clothed. Casey watched as the woman shot the stranger, rocking him back into the dry soil. She stepped forward and pulled the trigger again, this time cutting a hole through his thigh. He screamed and gripped his wounds, his face filled with rabid ferocity as he cursed them and promised them all a place in Hell beside him. The energy coursing through her made her heart stutter. She lowered her hands as the old man was forced into the trunk of his own car.

"Can you still see?" Javier asked.

"It's leaving me," Casey said.

She fell to her knees, devastated. "She's hurt... really bad. I feel terrible. Death is all around us. It lives here!"

"What about him? The man that has been hurting her?" Javier asked.

"They put him in the trunk of the car. I saw a fire in the distance—the church, I think."

Javier spoke the thought running through her mind, something she hesitated to admit, "I hope they kill that bastard. The evil in him will never cease until he's dead."

* * * *

Sixty-eight drove the old black car back to the flaming church. The other two women sat quietly, just praying for it all to be over. Celia held her broken arm against her chest. The agony of breathing told her that her ribs were more than likely shattered as well. Eighty-two laid her head back against the seat, her mouth and nose bled freely and her eyes were swollen nearly shut. As the preacher raged in the trunk, the sounds filled her with anxiety.

He wouldn't go down easy.

The church crackled with fire as it consumed the dry wooden walls. Sixty-eight brought the car to a stop and looked at her companions.

"We gotta get him in there. He ain't getting back out," she said. Her face was grim, her eyes ringed with dark circles.

Celia nodded, "I want to see him die."

The three women crawled from the car and stood at the trunk as the old man inside went wild again, pounding the trunk lid.

"Just put a bullet in his head," Eighty-two said, listening to him rage beyond the layer of steel between them.

"No. I want to watch him burn," Sixty-eight answered, checking the gun.

It only had two shots left. She would have to make them count.

* * * *

Sixty-eight kept the gun aimed at the trunk and nodded. Eighty-two slid the key in the lock and turned it. The lid flew open with a forceful kick from the preacher.

The minutes in the steel box had caused him to sweat from the oppressive desert heat. He was bleeding from his neck and two bullet wounds. Celia knew the gunshots weren't placed in fatal areas. It made her knees shake. The predator before them hadn't come so far by being a fool or succumbing to weakness. His eyes were wild as he sat up and came crawling from the trunk in a rage. Her fears were becoming reality as he charged towards Sixty-eight.

She pulled the trigger.

A bullet entered his chest and forced him back against the car. He fell to his knees as he struggled to breathe.

"Get in the church or I'll put one in your brain," The old woman threatened.

"Just shoot him," Celia said.

"No. He's gonna suffer first," Sixty-eight said wildly.

"Get on your goddamn feet," Eighty-two said.

The old man looked Sixty-eight dead in the eyes and sneered, "You can't kill me."

"Shut your mouth. You're not God! You're a man! And I'm gonna watch you die!" she screamed. Her arm shook as she pointed the gun at his head.

Byron stood, holding the bloody hole in his chest and staggering as she nudged him onward with the barrel of the gun. Eighty-two and Celia watched them as they approached the gaping mouth of fire that was once the church wall. The oldest of the prisoners was finally sending her tormentor to his death, becoming his executioner, a title she had always dreamed of attaining but never thought would become reality.

"Keep on walkin'," she said.

Byron surprised her by picking up speed. He ran into the flickering flames and disappeared in the inferno before her. The church swayed a bit as the fire fed on its support structure. It had never been strong to begin with, having been built by the hands of living ghosts.

Sixty-eight turned back to her companions, tears running down her cheeks. Celia watched her sway on her feet, relief coming out of her in a flood of weeping. With her back to the burning church, she was couldn't see the smoldering figure emerged from the inferno swinging a sledge hammer. He flattened the back of the old woman's head and her life was snuffed out in the blink of an eye.

Celia and Eighty-two ran for the car as the old man came for them, his hand fused to the steel handle of the burning hot sledge hammer. Hurling herself into the driver's seat, Celia turned the key and the car roared to life. She quickly threw it in gear and stomped on the gas. The doorway was near and she would carry them both through it, even if she had to run the old bastard over on her way out.

"Where did he go?" Eighty-two asked.

Byron was nowhere to be seen. It wasn't possible for him to simply disappear. Celia brought the car to a stop as they searched the surroundings. Anxiety gnawed at her. She wanted him dead more than anything.

The wall of the church crumpled outward as a flaming car came speeding out in reverse. Benjamin's car hadn't been destroyed by the slow burning fire. Byron came for them, demolition derby style, intent on stopping them from making it to the other side.

Celia jammed the pedal to the floor as the fiery car came slamming into them. They screamed and the old car rocked with the impact. Byron pulled the car forward, positioning it in an attempt to block the doorway but one of its front tires were already flat and the car didn't move as quickly as the bored-out black beast.

Celia kept the gas held to the floor. The car kicked up rooster tails of dust as it hurtled forward. She felt the doorway ahead, could see a faint outline. Focusing her mind, she felt the fire burning between her eyes. She prayed that Allan was right, that she could open the only exit from Hell in sight. Her head ached, her eyes rolled back into her skull, and she stiffened as they approached the doorway. Eighty-two screamed and threw her hands over her eyes.

The car entered the orb of darkness and came skidding out onto a black highway. Rust behind them came the mangled car of Benjamin, piloted by the preacher. He slammed into the back of his own car.

Clearing the black top, the two vehicles went careening into the desert off the shoulder of the road. The hammer was still melded to one of his hands, the skin of his palm permanently fused to it. Revving the engine, Byron slammed into them once more and drove them into a cactus. He opened the car door and climbed out, swinging his sledge hammer.

CHAPTER EIGHTEEN
ENDS AND BEGINNINGS

Casey was more exhausted and nauseated than when she had drank the *ayahuasca*. Her body was threatening to shut down. Javier helped her over to his car and sat her down in the front seat.

She couldn't speak for crying. Touching the doorway had been too intense for her, and watching her sister fighting for her life without being able to help felt like a punch in the stomach. Javier knelt in the dirt before her. He could feel her mind was nearly at the breaking point.

A roar filled the silent nighttime desert as a car came barreling out of the darkness, lightning crackling across it as it sped out of a hidden gateway. A second car followed close behind. Smoldering and windowless, it slammed into the black car ahead of it.

Javier shielded Casey as the two vehicles collided, then careened off the other side of the highway, coming to a stop in the decimated remains of a creosote bush.

Smoke danced around the wreckage as Javier approached it. The driver's side door of the battered black car swung open and a pale figure emerged. When his eyes fell on her, he knew who she had to be.

He jogged forward and quickly made his way down to the resting place of the two cars. He lifted his hands to show the frightened young woman that he meant her no harm. Behind her, came a second woman exiting the vehicle from the driver's side since her door was jammed in the splintered creosote bush.

"Are you ok?" Javier called to them.

He halted when they frantically scrambled. "I'm here to help you," he said.

"He's alive!" the young woman who looked like the mirror image of Casey screamed.

The door of the second car flew open. Javier took two steps back, watching as a charred man stepped out. In his hand, he wielded a sledge hammer, raising it to swing at the frightened women as they stumbled away from him.

"Leave them alone!" Javier yelled.

Their attacker stopped and slowly turned around to face Javier. The old man's skin was bubbled and burnt black across his chest. He snarled, baring his stained teeth, then he swung the hammer. Javier leapt back as it smashed into the side of the car beside him. The sandy soil slid out from under his feet and sent him falling onto his back.

Wheezing and coughing, the old man fought to bring the hammer up once more. Javier rolled over and crawled back towards the embankment. He looked up to see Casey standing there, her eyes wide, searching the scene before her.

"Run!" Javier cried.

"Look out!" Casey screamed and pointed.

Javier knew the old man was coming for a second attack. He rolled, luckily avoiding the blow of the heavy head of the hammer.

"Son of a bitch," Byron cursed just as something solid hit him in the back of the head, sending him tumbling forward.

Celia and Eighty-two were there with fists full of heavy rocks. Eighty-two launched a second stone that caught the preacher in the back as he tried to push himself back up.

Casey bent down at the shoulder of the highway and retrieved a few more rocks, then came down the small embankment firing them down on the back of the old man's head.

"Leave my sister alone!" she cried.

Celia looked in the direction of the dark-haired girl and her heart stuttered. It was the girl from her visions of freedom—her true other half. She hobbled slowly over as Javier and Eighty-two continued to bash Byron's skull with anything they could get their hands on.

"My sister?" she asked.

"Yes," Casey nodded and smiled through tears. "You're my sister."

Celia couldn't deny the resemblance, the dreams she had of finding herself on the dark highway. She embraced Casey and they continued to cry over the sounds of the old man's body being broken as he was stoned by the others.

Byron was completely still. Fresh blood trickled down over his burnt flesh. The hammer had torn free in his struggle, taking the meat of his palm with it.

When everything was silent and dawn began to lighten the horizon, Javier helped the three women into his car and they sped off down the desolate highway.

They left the old man there, a feast for the vultures and coyotes, as they made their way for the border.

****

Celia laid her head against her sister's shoulder and finally closed her eyes. Eighty-two sat in the back seat, her eyes taking in the real world as it passed them outside the station wagon window.

"Where are we gonna go?" Casey asked Javier, stroking her sister's hair.

"First, we're gonna get you all cleaned up at a rest stop, then I know a good place that you will find healing and a new life," he answered. "You'll all have to learn to speak Spanish, but you have the rest of your lives for that."

"Will you stay with us?" Casey asked.

"Of course. I owe my grandmother's brother a great deal for when he saved my life. I want to learn from him and continue his work. It was a promise I made to him long ago."

She smiled and looked down to Celia. "When she wakes up, I will tell her all about Annemarie."

"Annemarie?" Eighty-two asked. "That was my sister's name."

She sat forward as Casey turned back to her, tears filled Eighty-two's eyes as realization washed over her.

"We are family," she whispered.

* * * *

Dawn slowly warmed the black top as he crawled across it. He didn't care how it bit his skin. There was hardly any of it left. Byron expended the last of his energy making his way on his hands and knees to the doorway before falling through on his face. His lungs felt as if they were constricting. His chest burned. He fell forward into the desert sand. Death was coming for him, there was no way around it.

The scent of the smoldering church comforted him in a way. It had always been more of a home to him than any other place... even the house he shared with Betty.

The highway patrol would find the wreckage and assume that he had wandered into the desert in confusion. Betty would be torn apart by it, but there was no way he could think of getting around his fate.

It was nighttime in the nowhere desert, but it hadn't occurred to him that the hunters would be scavenging until shadowy hands flipped him over. Its bright eyes gazed down at him as he drew a last deep breath.

He waited for it to plunge its dark fist into his abdomen and use its claws to tear through his charred hide to seek his heart, their favorite morsel. It sniffed and chuffed, tasting the air between them. A thick rope of drool slid from its mouth, but it didn't strike. It backed away and fled as he felt a surge of some new power rush through him.

Byron lifted a charred hand, and in the darkness he watched it pulling and stretching, long black claws forcing themselves painfully out through his fingertips. He rose to his knees, screaming as he felt like his insides were beginning to boil. Falling forward, he retched as his body contorted.

He climbed to his feet, realizing that his lungs would not fill with breath. His payment for living the life of a monster was being dealt to him tenfold. He would now become one of them, doomed to hunt in the shadows.

He ran for his church, now nothing but ashes and glowing embers, like the skeleton of a burnt creature that had lain down to die in the desert. Placing his deformed hand over his chest where his heart struggled to beat, he felt a hunger filling him, uncontrollable in its ferocity.

The green light of the doorway called to him. He ran for it, knowing somehow that once the painful transformation was complete, he would be trapped in this desert in the middle of nowhere.

He wondered if Betty had dinner waiting for him ...if she would be waiting as she always did.

★ ★ ★ ★

The roar of his engine sounded off. She looked out the window to see the black car falter as it met the sidewalk out front. It was dented terribly and smoke roiled from under the hood.

"Byron?" Betty whispered her voice hoarse. "My goodness."

She could see his bent shadow hobbling up the walkway, so she left the window to open the door for him. She had waited all night, and called every hospital around and his brother seven times, but she hadn't been able to locate her missing husband.

Opening the front door, she nearly fainted to see him bleeding, filthy, his skin blackened and peeling. Betty pulled him inside and shut the door in hysteria.

"Let me help you lay down then I'm calling the doctor! What happened to you?"

She helped him stumble to his favorite chair then flipped on the lamp beside the coffee table. Her hands shook so badly that she could hardly locate the telephone she always left within reach in case Byron tried to call her.

"*Hungry...,*" he answered.

"I'll fix you some food as soon as the doctor sees you," she said, lifting the phone to her face and squinting to see the numbers.

She thumbed the call button, but before she could dial 9-1-1, a hand fell on her shoulder. Its fingers were long and twisted, with razor-sharp nails at their tips. She was spun roughly around and the lamp beside the phone tipped over, shining brightly on her injured husband. Illuminated his face, she saw a visage that was changing before her eyes, morphing into something of nightmares.

She tried to scream but his fist was there first, forcing its way down her throat and seeking the beating organ in her chest.

THE END

ABOUT THE AUTHORS

Melissa Lason and Michelle Garza have been writing together since they were little girls. Dubbed *The Sisters of Slaughter* by the editors of Fireside Press, they are constantly working together on new stories in the horror and dark fantasy genres. Their work has been included in FRESH MEAT published by Sinister Grin Press, WISHFUL THINKING by Fireside Press, as well as WIDOWMAKERS a benefit anthology of dark fiction.

Follow them on Facebook & Twitter

https://facebook.com/sistersofhorror/

https://twitter.com/fiendbooks

WELCOME TO THE BLACK
MOUNTAIN CAMP FOR BOYS!

Summer,1989. It is a time for splashing in the lake and exploring the wilderness, for nine teenagers to bond together and create friendships that could last the rest of their lives.

But among this group there is a young man with a secret--a secret that, in this time and place, is unthinkable to his peers.
When the others discover the truth, it will change each of them forever. They will all have blood on their hands.

ODD MAN OUT is a heart-wrenching tale of bullies and bigotry, a story that explores what happens when good people don't stand up for what's right. It is a tale of how far we have come . . . and how far we still have left to go.

Available in paperback or Kindle on Amazon.com

ISBN-13: 978-0998067919

Welcome to the small Midwestern town of Belford, Ohio. It's summer vacation and fourteen-year-old Toby Fairchild is looking forward to spending a lazy, carefree summer playing basketball, staying up late watching monster movies, and camping out in his backyard with his best friend, Frankie.

But then tragedy strikes. And out of this tragedy an unlikely friendship develops between Toby and the local bogeyman, a strange old man across the street named Mr. Joseph. Over the course of a tumultuous summer, Toby will be faced with pain and death, the excitement of his first love, and the underlying racism of the townsfolk, all while learning about the value of freedom at the hands of a kind but cursed old man.

Every town has a dark side. And in Belford, the local bogeyman has a story to tell.

Available in paperback or Kindle on Amazon.com

ISBN-13: 978-0692730980

The empty airwaves of the mind...

Welcome to TunnelVision – the premium channel streaming from the imagination of R. Patrick Gates to you!

What happens when you lose sight of the forest for the trees?

Wilbur Clayton has a personal connection with Jesus – Murder! Abused for most of his life, Wilbur and Jesus are out to make amends and take revenge. With Grandma in his head and Jesus on the TunnelVision, Wilbur knows what must be done and who must be made to pay for the sins of the father...

The only thing standing in his way are a cop with a gift for details and deduction, and a young genius whose reenactments of his favorite books are about to become all too real.

TunnelVision – streaming seven days a week, 24 hours a day!

On the air and in your nightmares!

Available in paperback or Kindle on Amazon.com

ISBN-13: 978-0998067902

I KNOW WHAT YOU HAVE HEARD ABOUT ME

You say that I am a madman. You say that I am dangerous. You say that I am the one who has been abducting women, slaughtering them, and burying their corpses all around this city for years. You are wrong, because only part of that statement is true...

I AM NOT A KILLER

I know that you probably won't believe me. Not now. Not after all that has happened, but I need to tell my side of the story. You need to know how this all began. You need to hear about the birds, but most of all, you need to understand...

I AM NOT THE BOULEVARD MONSTER

Available in paperback or Kindle on Amazon.com

ISBN-13: 978-0998067957

A NUCLEAR STORM POURS DOWN
FROM THE HEAVENS

A global disaster strikes suddenly when the Space Shuttle explodes over the Atlantic seaboard, unleashing its toxic payload over thousands of miles. Millions flee. Millions more perish in the deluge . . . and they are the lucky ones. Those who do not die immediately after exposure soon sicken and succumb in horrific agony.

ON SEA BREEZE ISLAND, A PLAGUE OF
UNDEATH REANIMATES THE FALLEN

Their minds still function, but their flesh continues to bloat and decay. Ostracized by the fortunate few who have escaped the radioactive rain and quarantined to the water's edge, the "Beachers" are treated as inhuman monsters by family and friends; soon they will become as loathsome in behavior as they are in appearance.

For one particular survivor – a single mother named Sandy – the monster is very familiar. He will put her through a Hell beyond her darkest nightmares, but in order to protect her child, she will endure and do anything. Absolutely anything.

Available in paperback or Kindle on Amazon.com

ISBN-13: 978-0998067957

A MAN IN MOURNING

Still haunted by the death of his wife two years earlier, Derrick Grayson travels with his gifted son Nathan to her hometown of Moss Creek. There, he reunites with her mother, Grace, hoping to bring some peace to his broken heart and to give Nathan a normal childhood.

A TOWN UNDER THE SHADOW OF EVIL

Moss Creek harbors a dark secret, though. Local children have been disappearing for decades, with no trace of them ever found. When a swath of slaughter and bloodshed cuts its way through the townspeople and Derrick finds himself directly in its path, he must join with a group of kindred souls to hunt down the malevolent specter behind the carnage... a dark figure from a twisted shadowy realm... An ancient unearthly entity known as...

THE RAGGEDY MAN

Available in paperback or Kindle on Amazon.com

ISBN-13: 978-0998067988

A TERRIFYING HAUNTING

This is the place where the harrowed ghosts of a dozen generations whisper in the shadows of their ancestral home, where one family's dreams of a new beginning turned into a nightmare that ended in tragedy.

A CURSED BLOODLINE

This is the place where a line of witches bound themselves—in blood—to a primeval entity. Here, nightmare and reality meet beneath frozen skies, and even time and space fall under the power of the demonic being that rules this remote northern wood.

A CHANCE ENCOUNTER

This is the place where the path of a tormented survivor meets that of an unknowing innocent. Past and present collide, and secrets long buried crawl back into the pallid light of day as the shadow of the Beast falls over them both. But even the bloodiest dreams of that demonic being may pale in comparison to what lies buried within the human heart.

This is the place where evil dwells ...

ABODE

Available in paperback or Kindle on Amazon.com

ISBN-13: 978-0998067988

ON THE HORIZON FROM
BLOODSHOT BOOKS

2017*

Sinkhole – Ken Goldman
Dust to Dust – M.C. Norris
White Death – Christine Morgan
Red Diamond – Michales Joy
The Organ Donor – Matthew Warner
What Hides Within – Jason Parent
It Sustains – Mark Morris
Shadow Child: 30th Anniversay Edition – Joseph Citro
The Noctuary: Pandemonium – Greg Chapman

2018*

Victoria (What Hides Within #2) – Jason Parent
Happy Cage – Gene Lazuta
The Winter Tree – Mark Morris
Blood Mother: A Novel of Terror – Pete Kahle
Not Your Average Monster, Volume 3
Practitioners – Matt Heyward & Patrick Lacey

2019-20*

The Abomination (The Riders Saga #2) – Pete Kahle
The Horsemen (The Riders Saga #3) – Pete Kahle
Not Your Average Monster, Volume 4

* other titles to be added when confirmed

BLOODSHOT BOOKS

READ UNTIL
YOU BLEED!

CPSIA information can be obtained
at www.ICGtesting.com
Printed in the USA
LVOW03s0019040418
572237LV00001B/176/P